Ladies

Story Of A Mission Accomplished - Sort Of

Marcia Allen Bennett

Outskirts Press, Inc.
Denver, Colorado

This is a work of fiction. The events and characters described herein are imaginary and are not intended to refer to specific places or living persons. The opinions expressed in this manuscript are solely the opinions of the author and do not represent the opinions or thoughts of the publisher.

Ladies of the Bomb Squad
Story Of A Mission Accomplished - Sort Of
All Rights Reserved.
Copyright © 2008 Marcia Allen Bennett
V3.0

Cover Photo © 2008 JupiterImages Corporation. All rights reserved - used with permission.

This book may not be reproduced, transmitted, or stored in whole or in part by any means, including graphic, electronic, or mechanical without the express written consent of the publisher except in the case of brief quotations embodied in critical articles and reviews.

Outskirts Press, Inc.
http://www.outskirtspress.com

ISBN: 978-1-4327-2067-4

Outskirts Press and the "OP" logo are trademarks belonging to Outskirts Press, Inc.

PRINTED IN THE UNITED STATES OF AMERICA

Dedication

To my fellow travelers in this stage of life who face the adversities of old age with courage, grace, and a full measure of laughter.

Acknowledgments

Thanks to all of you, my children, for your support of all my projects. A special thanks to my daughter Carol Ann for her encouragement, her suggestions, and for putting her time and heart into editing this book.

CHAPTER One

Crackling with fury, Evie finished dealing the cards, then slammed her own cards down on the table.

"Let's blow it up!"

"What?" Bertha gasped. "Blow it up?"

"Sure. It seems an appropriate way to get rid of the danged thing."

Bertha sneered at Evie, "Don't you think blowing it up is a bit drastic?"

"No, I do not. I moved into this place hoping for some peace and quiet and every stinking day they are running one of those 10,000-decibel machines. We pay an arm and a leg to live in this retirement complex and this is what they do to us. I'm sick and tired of it. And it's every day. I keep track of it.

"Monday, the walkways; Tuesday, the parking lot; Wednesday, the balconies; then Thursday...well, you know the drill."

Sally sighed. "Guess they never heard of a broom."

"Don't butt in, Sally. I'm not through with my story. Let's see, where was I? Oh, yes, today here comes Rudy with the leaf blower roaring right outside our apartment doors. I'm telling you, all the devil needs to make it truly hell is one of those leaf blowers."

"Well, Evie," said Sally, "you have to admit the balconies needed blowing. I took a walk out there this morning and actually saw two leaves. Heaven forbid those two leaves be swept away with a nice, quiet broom."

The foursome's Friday bridge game in the activity room of The Gardendale had become as much a part of their lives as mealtimes or their Tuesday excursions to the grocery store. However, their bantering conversation had slammed to an abrupt halt as the leaf blower wielded by one of the maintenance staff made its noisy way down the walkway just outside the activity room.

Melba studied her hand for a moment, then folded her cards together. "I'm ready to do something drastic, too. Sometimes I feel like I'm living in the middle of an O'Hare Airport runway instead of a retirement center. I'm with Evie. Let's blow up every leaf blower we can find in this place."

Sally absently-mindedly fanned out the cards in her hand, then re-folded them and laid them face down on the table in front of her. "You know, of course, that I have discussed this noise problem with the management and with quite a few of the other residents. The people in the office just shrug like they can't do anything about it and most of the residents don't seem to care much one way or the other. Problem is that since so many of them are already deaf as posts, the noise doesn't bother them."

"That's for sure," agreed Evie. "Have you ever tried to have a conversation with Maizie? Lordy mercy, it'll wear you to a nub. 'Maizie, you look really pretty today.' 'No, I'm not going to the city for hay.' And it goes downhill from there."

Sally continued, "What I'm saying is you can't find many residents who care enough about the noise to do anything about it. So if anybody blows up the stuff, we're the ones who will have to do it. First thing we need to do is find out how to make a bomb. Anybody know how to do that?"

"Oh, sure, just mix up a little TNT and some dynamite!" laughed Bertha. "You three are crazy, talking like we are really going to blow up that equipment."

"Well, I think we should do it," said Evie. "Maybe we could just set it on fire. The leaf blower has a gasoline engine, so if we set it on fire, it would probably blow up."

"Maybe we could just steal it and hide it in the dumpster," Bertha suggested.

"They'd only buy another one, probably an even noisier one," Sally said with resignation. "We have to blow this one up to make a statement just like in a real protest."

"Sally, what do you know about a 'real protest'? Did you ever participate in one in your whole life?"

"Well, yes, I did, Bertha. I participated in a boycott of my high school cafeteria to protest the horrible food they served. So there."

"Yes, but did anybody get arrested? It's not a real protest unless somebody gets arrested and hauled off to jail."

Melba jumped in. "Let's quit arguing about protests and get on with our bridge game. We can figure out later how we're going to bomb that leaf blower." The four friends played quietly until the game ended.

"Okay, everybody," said Melba, gathering up the cards as the others folded the chairs and leaned them against the activity room wall, "the Bomb Squad will meet in my apartment Monday afternoon and see what we can come up with."

CHAPTER TWO

Bertha and Sally sat on the sofa as Evie settled herself in the swivel rocker in Melba's apartment.

Melba put a plate of Oreos on the coffee table and moved her walker to the remaining chair. She lowered herself carefully onto the seat cushion. "Okay, everybody has coffee and I've put the cookies where you can reach them, so let's get down to business. I'll start. I think I should be the one to plant the bomb on the leaf blower. Here's what I'll..."

Evie interrupted. "Melba, you are the last person in the world who ought to be setting off a bomb. You mess up everything you try to cook because you forget to set the timer or you don't follow the directions, half the time we have to remind you to come to the dining room to eat, and as slow as you are with that walker, you couldn't even get away before the bomb blew up. Face it. You are just a sweet little old lady who wouldn't harm a flea."

"That's 'fly,' Evie, not 'flea,'" corrected Bertha. Evie glared at her.

"Flea, fly, who cares?" exclaimed Melba. "Did you all hear what Evie just said? About how slow and forgetful and ditzy I am? She just made my argument for me. All those are reasons they would never suspect me."

"You know what?" said Sally. "She's right. Nobody would ever think a sweet person like Melba would set off a bomb. Melba's perfect for the job."

"Yes, but that part about your not being able to get away before it blows. What about that?" asked Bertha.

"No problem," answered Melba. "I'll just put a long fuse on it or set the timer way ahead or whatever it is they do with bombs. And I promise I won't make a very big bomb. It only has to be big enough to mess up the leaf blower. It'll be easy."

"You say it's easy, but it seems to me we are back to square one," said Sally. "We have no idea how to make a bomb."

"That's where you are wrong." Melba picked up an envelope from the table beside her. "Here are all the directions we need. And the instructions don't call for anything weird like plastic explosives or such. Most of the ingredients are stuff that's easy to get hold of."

Sally paled and almost choked on her coffee. "Where in the world did you get directions for making a bomb?"

"It was no problem. Over the weekend I called

my son Ryan, you know, the one who's a chef. I remembered that he learned something about bombs in the Army. I told him I was writing a mystery story and needed to know how to make a simple bomb." She chuckled. "And he bought it, hook, line, and sinker. I wrote the directions down exactly as he told them to me and they are right here in this envelope. I was surprised at how easy it is to make a bomb."

Evie reached for the envelope. "Let's see what it takes to make a bomb."

"Oh, no. No way," said Melba, clutching the envelope to her chest. "I am going to be the only one who will know what goes into this bomb. That way, if any of you are caught and tortured, you won't know anything that could get you into trouble."

"But, Melba," protested Evie, "we are all in this together. We should at least see what goes into the bomb."

"Absolutely not," Melba said. "I am putting my foot down on this. I will be the ONLY one who knows what goes into the bomb."

"But what about getting hold of the stuff to make it? Won't you need our help?" asked Bertha.

"There's only one item that could be a little tricky to get hold of, but I think I can manage that."

"I just don't feel right about your making this bomb all by yourself." Sally sighed. "But if you insist, I guess we have no choice. However, there's something else we have to work out. How are we going to steal the leaf blower and the power washer?"

"Don't you think," asked Melba, "that we should just deal with the leaf blower? If we blow it up, we'll be making enough of a protest statement."

"You're right, Melba," Sally said after a moment's thought. "No need for us to try to destroy every noisy object in this place. So let's get on with how we can steal the leaf blower."

"I've been thinking about that," said Evie. "I have that big roller suitcase I use when I visit my daughter in Colorado. That thing not only holds all my clothes, but it also has room for a two-week supply of bulky Depends underwear, so I have no doubt at all that it will hold the leaf blower. You see people dragging suitcases around here all the time so nobody would think anything about it. I could dress up like I do when I am going on a trip, with my purse and everything. Everybody would just think I'm headed out of town again. What do you think?"

"But somebody is bound to ask you where you're going. And then what will you say?"

"Well, Bertha, I'm not going to lie. I'll say, 'Oh, just a quick trip, but I have some really bulky items I have to carry.' If I'm lucky, I won't have to say more."

"Okay, Evie, we know what to put the stolen object in, but when and how can we actually steal it?"

Before Evie could answer, Melba spoke up. "We need to case the joint. We can start our surveillance of the leaf blower right away. Whenever we hear it we can take a walk around the property and check things out. Here, everybody--I'll pass around this package of earplugs. Keep some with you at all times and report back to me whenever you have surveilled the leaf blower."

Sally suppressed a giggle. "You sound like somebody in one of those crime shows on TV."

"Well, why not? Aren't we plotting to commit a crime?"

Evie shuddered. "Don't say that. I have convinced myself that we really are trying to do a good deed and save people from stress and loss of hearing."

"Hey, I like that!" Bertha helped herself to another Oreo. "I was having a little trouble with my conscience, too, but thinking of it that way makes me feel better."

"Back to our surveillance," said Melba. "I seem to remember seeing the maintenance man go to lunch and leave the blower beside a bush or half hidden somewhere until he finishes lunch. Maybe he doesn't always go all the way back to the maintenance shed to put the thing away. We just need to be sure."

Melba took a sip of her coffee and placed the cup back into the saucer on the table beside her. "Okay, then," she continued, "our assignment for this week is surveillance of the leaf blower. Let's meet back here next Monday and compare notes. Meanwhile, I'll gather the ingredients for the bomb so I'll have everything ready to go."

Sally and Evie walked with Bertha to her apartment, then headed to their courtyard.

"Sally, I am really worried about Melba doing all this bomb building by herself. In fact, I worry about her anyway. I'm sure you've noticed that sometimes she seems to be out of touch with reality. I don't see how she can play bridge so well and yet be so absent-minded and addled in other ways."

"I'd be worried, too, Evie, except that I've seen this before in old people. Maybe it's because Melba has been playing bridge all her adult life and all that practice keeps her brain in gear for that particular activity."

"I guess you're right. You've made me feel better. I just hope she's okay and there's nothing wrong with her." Evie entered her apartment with a wave goodbye and Sally continued along the balcony to her own apartment.

When she reached the door, she stood staring at it, key in hand. She somehow couldn't make herself push her hand to put the key into the lock. She thrust the key back into her pocket and headed for the elevator. She needed to think and the best place for that was her favorite bench in the rose garden. Sally had a decision to make and it was eating her up.

CHAPTER Three

That same evening Melba started worrying about the bomb and realized that Ryan hadn't mentioned a detonator. In all the TV shows, the bomb always had a detonator. She picked up her phone and punched in his number.

"Hey, Ryan. It's Mom. How are you?"

"Everything's great here, Mom. How goes it with you?"

"Everything is just fine with me, too. Those new vitamins you suggested really help. Uh, Ryan, I've been thinking about the story I'm writing, you remember, the one with the bomb. You didn't tell me anything about detonating the thing. How would the person do that?"

"Decorating it? Oh, just put a candle on top and light it when the time comes. What's going on? It sounds more like you are celebrating somebody's birthday than writing a mystery story!"

Melba was puzzled at the odd comment. "No, nobody's birthday. Ryan, are you sure these directions will make a good bomb?"

"Absolutely, Mom, the best one you can imagine. Have fun writing your mystery story. I can't wait to read it."

Melba hung up the phone. She trusted Ryan to have given her an accurate list of the items needed and the correct directions for putting the bomb together, but she couldn't imagine how such commonplace items could make a bomb. It just seemed too easy. It was scary to think that anybody and everybody could make a bomb with these directions. She made up her mind that when this was all over, she would destroy the directions so no one else would ever use them to make such a destructive weapon.

She thought about the candle Ryan had told her to use. Obviously the wick was the fuse and the candle would burn down slowly enough for her to get away. Just to be on the safe side, she would buy some of those candles that are bigger than dinky little birthday cake candles. She wanted to have plenty of time to make her getaway before the thing blew. All she had to do now was get the candles.

Then Melba remembered one more thing she needed, something very important. She had spent hours on the phone calling shops and stores trying to find the bomb mold that Ryan had told her to use. Finally, at a junky antique store in a not-so-nice part of town, she located a bomb mold and asked the owner to put it aside for her until she could get there. "I'll take a cab to the shop on Saturday morning," she told him, "so please don't sell the bomb mold to anybody else." The storeowner assured her he would have her package all ready for her when she arrived. Meanwhile, she sure hoped some government spy agency wasn't listening in to her phone calls.

*****

The Bomb Squad gathered in Melba's apartment on Monday. After serving coffee and putting a plate of chocolate chip cookies on the coffee table, Melba sat down and took a clipboard and pen from the seat of her walker.

"I'm ready for reports on the leaf blower surveillance," she announced.

Sally spoke first. "Every time I heard any kind of blower, I left the apartment to follow up on it. I didn't have much luck, though. Rudy was using it most of the time and he seems to be very conscientious about putting it away when he is finished with it. What about you, Evie?"

"Same thing. I must admit, though, that I didn't go out every time I heard the leaf blower. It hurts my ears even with the earplugs."

Bertha was squirming in her seat and with a satisfied smile said, "I had better luck than you did. I went out every time I heard that monster roaring, and one of those times I surveilled the new guy in maintenance, I think his name is Clyde. It was close to lunchtime so I kept a close eye on him. Sure enough, when it was time to eat, he hid the blower behind the swimming pool equipment shed and off he went to lunch."

"That would be a perfect place for us to pick up the blower," said Evie, "because the pool equipment shed is off in a corner and hidden by shrubbery. Nobody would see us. But the problem is that Rudy is the one who does most of the leaf blowing, not the new man."

"No problem!" Bertha was gleeful. "I overheard Rudy telling one of the housekeepers that he'll be away on vacation all next week. Bet you anything the new guy will be the one using the leaf blower."

"Hot ziggity!" Evie raised a fist in the air. "We're in business. Looks like our plan is coming together. Melba, how about the stuff to make the bomb? Do you have everything?"

"I just needed one more item and I had a lot of trouble finding it. I was able to get all the other things on the shopping trips our Activities Director takes us on. But this one item is really important and I had to take a cab to a special place to buy it. But I have that item now and I have everything else I need to make the bomb!"

"Can't you even tell us what that one item is?" asked Bertha. "My curiosity is getting the best of me."

"Nope. As they say in the business, 'if I told you I would have to kill you.'"

"Melba, you definitely have been watching too many crime shows on TV," Bertha replied.

"Maybe, but you can learn a lot from those shows. Back to our bomb--why don't we plan to blow up the leaf blower next Monday? They always clean the walkways off after a weekend, so there's a good chance the blower will be used.

"Bertha, you have a cell phone so you go with Evie to steal the blower and put it in the suitcase. When you have the leaf blower safely stashed in the suitcase, call me on your cell phone to be sure the coast is clear. If I give you the all clear, then Evie can wheel the suitcase to my apartment."

"Gotcha." said Bertha. "Then when it's dark, Sally can help you get the blower to the far corner of the property where you two will blow it up."

"Okay," said Melba, "Sally can help get the blower over there, but I am setting up the bomb myself. I'll just get nervous if anybody is watching me, and it will be better if there is only one of us out there anyway. So, Sally, set your alarm for 2 a.m. Tuesday morning and we'll move that leaf blower to the bomb site. Oh, and be sure to wear dark clothing. Your black pants and that black top with the hood would be perfect."

Sally reluctantly agreed to the plan. "Okay, I'll wear black clothes, but I still think you should let me help you set up the bomb."

"Nope, no way, so forget it."

CHAPTER Four

Stealing the leaf blower proved to be no problem at all for Evie and Bertha. Bertha was keeping watch and sure enough, at lunchtime the new maintenance man shoved the blower under a shrub behind the pool equipment shed and left it while he went to eat. Bertha phoned Evie. "Hurry. Bring the suitcase to the equipment shed."

In what seemed only moments, Evie showed up, pulling the bulky black piece of luggage behind her. She opened it up and pulled out a big beach towel. "I don't want that dirty thing ruining my suitcase," she explained as she wrapped the blower in the towel. The two women then quickly stuffed the blower inside the suitcase.

Bertha dialed Melba's number. "Mission accomplished."

"Copy that," Melba answered. "All clear here.

Ten four. Over and out."

"We had better not both go to Melba's," Bertha whispered to Evie. "It could look suspicious. Can you manage the suitcase alone?"

"Sure, no problem at all." Evie shoved her purse back up on her shoulder and made her way through the courtyard to Melba's apartment.

Melba greeted her at the door. "Quick. Come in. I've been watching for you. Any problems? Any nosy neighbors or security people lurking around out there?"

"Nope. Our assignment went well. I hope yours will go as smoothly."

"Me, too. Wish me luck tonight."

*****

As the evening wore on, Melba was so nervous that she didn't even bother to get undressed for bed. She knew there was no way she would sleep. She donned her black pants and favorite black knit top, then dug around in a dresser drawer until she found a black scarf to tie over her white hair. Since all her comfortable shoes were light-colored, she would have to wear her dressy black patent leather pumps. I hope these shiny shoes don't reflect the light and get us caught, Melba thought to herself as she slipped them on. The heels were higher than she remembered and she tottered unsteadily. She was grateful she would have her walker to hang on to while she transported the bomb.

Melba read for a while, then watched TV, then read some more. Promptly at 2 a.m., she heard a soft tap at the door. She opened the door a crack, then grabbed Sally's arm and pulled her in. Melba whispered, "You take the suitcase. I've got the bomb in a box on the seat of my walker. Let's go!"

Sally gulped at the word "bomb." They were really going to do this and it was scarier than she expected. Closing the door quietly behind them, they made their way to the parking lot, Sally pulling the suitcase and Melba pushing her walker. Suddenly Melba stopped and gasped. "Oh, no!"

"What's wrong?" Sally asked shakily.

"I forgot about the security cameras, that's what's wrong," she whispered. "Don't you remember? They have new security cameras set up on all the parking lots and they'll see us and then what will we do? Oh, dear, oh, dear." Melba was standing at the edge of the parking lot, wringing her hands as she teetered on her high heels.

Sally took Melba's hands in hers. "Not to worry. Trust me on this. I was in the back office a few days ago and saw where the monitors are for the security cameras. Since they have cut down on security staff, there's nobody to sit in that little closet during the night and watch the cameras. They have to have somebody at the front desk all night long so I don't know how the cameras do anything more than give a false sense of security. We'll be just fine. Trust me. Nobody is watching those monitors."

"That makes sense; with so few security people,

who's going to sit around and look at monitors all night long? Okay, then, let's go."

The two women then tiptoed across the parking lot toward the far corner, Melba often tottering uneasily in her Sunday shoes. "Boy, it's hard to keep this darned suitcase quiet," Sally said, easing the piece of luggage over a bump in the pavement.

"I know," whispered Melba. "I feel like this walker has a loudspeaker attached to it, broadcasting every little squeak and rattle to the world. Why didn't I think to oil the wheels? Let's just hope everybody is sound asleep."

"Shh. Wait a minute. Listen."

Melba froze. "What is it?" she whispered.

"Footsteps. Over near the dumpster. Can you hear them?"

"Yes. Oh, my gosh, I do hear them. And I think they are getting closer. Sally, what are we going to do?"

"I say let's just stand where we are until we see who it is. If it's not the security guard, we may be okay."

The two women stood as still as though they had been turned into pillars of salt. Sally finally took her courage in hand and looked slowly over her shoulder. "Oh, thank heaven! It's Emmaline, that poor woman they call the 'night walker.'"

"Oh, I can breathe again. Poor Emmaline. She desperately needs a 24-hour caregiver or maybe just one at night to be sure she doesn't leave her apartment."

"Yeah. That sleep-walking can be dangerous;

she could get hurt. But so far, when she does this she finds her way back to her apartment, goes back to bed, and never remembers a thing about being anywhere but snug in her bed all night long."

"Well, she's heading back toward her apartment so I guess we can get on with our business."

When they reached the area they had selected, Sally opened the suitcase, carefully removed the leaf blower, and placed it on the ground.

"Okay, that's good," said Melba. "Now you take the suitcase back to your place. I'll get the bomb set up on top of the leaf blower, and then, BOOM! By the time this thing blows, I'll be safely back in my apartment. I'll see you at breakfast in the morning."

"Are you sure you'll be okay?"

"Of course, just go. Hurry up! I need to get this thing all set up and I need you gone before I do it."

Sally did as she was told, although she hated to leave Melba. "That's one stubborn woman," she muttered softly as she tiptoed noiselessly back to her apartment.

*****

The next morning, the four friends went to their usual table in a far corner of the dining room and sat down hurriedly, anxious to review their crime over breakfast.

"Okay, everybody," whispered Bertha. "Let's talk softly and be careful that nobody overhears us. First of all, did any of you hear the thing go off this morning?"

"No, I didn't hear a sound and I stayed awake listening for it," said Melba.

"So did I," said Sally, "and I never heard it, either. Maybe it didn't go off. Melba, are you sure you followed the directions exactly?"

"Of course I did," answered Melba, insulted by the implication. "I did everything exactly according to the directions."

"Well, we can't go check it out. If anybody saw us heading to that corner, it would be a dead giveaway that we were involved."

"Oh, rats," said Evie, dejectedly. "All that planning and work and the bomb probably didn't even go off. I guess we lost that battle."

*****

Later that morning, Melba, Sally, Evie, and Bertha joined the other residents in the Community Center of the apartment complex for a special called meeting of the residents. The lively chatter died down as Sam Jones, Administrator of The Gardendale, marched to the front of the room and removed the microphone from its stand, then tapped the microphone: "Testing, testing. Okay, it's live. Can you hear me in the back? Good.

"I have called this meeting because of an incident that happened last night and which needs to be addressed. Someone stole our leaf blower, took it to an isolated corner of the property and left it there. One of the maintenance staff found it this morning intact, but covered with a sticky substance, which seeped into the motor and ruined the equipment.

"I know some of you have complained about the noise of the leaf blower. We have reason to believe that two of our own residents committed this act of vandalism. As you know, we have security cameras in place, but unfortunately when we reviewed the tape this morning, we could only make out two shadowy figures, not enough to help us identify the culprits. However, we do have a witness, a resident whose dog needed to go out very early this morning."

The four friends sat stone-faced as they listened, but Melba's hands were trembling.

"We thought about calling the police, but after discussing it further, the staff decided not to prosecute. We are aware that there have been complaints about the leaf blower. As we talked, Margo, our resident counselor, suggested that perhaps this act was meant to send a strong message about the noise of this piece of equipment. After some discussion, the rest of us concurred.

"We in no way condone this kind of behavior which is indeed criminal, but I am happy to announce that no charges will be brought against the perpetrators. Additionally, we are purchasing a new blower, one which is guaranteed to be quieter and less offensive than the damaged one. Are there any questions? No? Then the meeting is adjourned."

The four friends breathed a sigh of relief.

"Come on up to my apartment," said Melba,

"and let's celebrate with a cup of tea."

"And I think you should finally show us the instructions for the bomb that made a sticky mess and ruined the leaf blower," Bertha said.

In Melba's apartment they sipped their tea. Melba opened the drawer of the table beside her. "Okay, here are the bomb directions, but as soon as you have looked at this, I am going to shred it and flush it down the toilet so nobody else can ever use it to make a bomb." Melba handed the envelope to Bertha. "You'll see that the item that was so difficult to find was the bomb mold."

Bertha opened the envelope eagerly and unfolded the piece of paper inside. As she read Melba's careful printing, her eyes grew large and she struggled to contain her laughter. She could hold it no longer and began laughing so hard that she couldn't speak. She passed the paper to Evie, who also erupted into laughter.

"What is it? What is so funny?" asked Melba.

"Oh, dear, sweet Melba," answered Bertha, with tears running down her cheeks. "This isn't a recipe for a bomb. It's a recipe for a bombe! A bombe is a fancy frozen ice cream dessert. Your son gave you a recipe for a dessert which is frozen in a bombe mold."

Melba's eyes lighted up. "That explains the candle, and the ingredients, which did seem odd for a bomb, and why Ryan asked me if it was somebody's birthday. I can't believe I made a dessert when I thought I was making a bomb." She sighed. "And all that delicious ice cream wasted on a leaf blower!"

*****

RYAN'S THREE-LAYERED BOMBE RECIPE

Ingredients:
1 quart French vanilla ice cream
1 quart coffee ice cream
1 quart buttered pecan ice cream
1/2 cup toasted pecans, finely chopped

Directions:
1. Lightly coat a 3-quart bombe mold or metal bowl with vegetable oil or spray. Chill in freezer one hour.
2. Put French vanilla ice cream in refrigerator for about an hour or until softened. Working quickly, push ice cream into bottom and sides of mold. Lay plastic wrap tightly onto ice cream and return mold to freezer.
3. Then soften the coffee ice cream the same way and spread it over the French vanilla after removing the plastic wrap. Cover the coffee ice cream layer with plastic wrap and put in freezer.
4. Soften buttered pecan ice cream and fill center of mold with it. Cover with plastic wrap and return to freezer for at least four hours.
5. To unmold, dip mold quickly into lukewarm water and invert onto chilled platter. Pat chopped pecans onto top of bombe. Return to freezer until ready to use.

CHAPTER Five

The merciless Texas sun beating down on the black asphalt of the Gardendale parking lot sent waves of heat onto the small group of residents standing in the corner of the property.

"It would have been thoughtful of the management to schedule this fire drill sometime other than the middle of the afternoon of the hottest day of the year," complained Glenna, a new Gardendale resident. "I know poor little Bootsie is suffering." She stroked the fur of the gray toy poodle she held in her arms. "I'm ready for the all-clear to sound. It's miserable out here. We could all die of heat stroke."

"It is unseasonably warm," agreed Bertha, obviously irritated by Glenna's complaints, "but wait until summer comes. Then you'll see what a hot day in Texas is *really* like. Besides, I'm more worried about who *isn't* out here. Where is Lucy? I know she is at home this morning because I saw her at the mailbox a few minutes before the alarm sounded and she was headed home to polish her shoes."

"Polish her shoes? She told you that?"

"Uh, huh. She has to wear those ugly black lace-up things she hates so she says the least she can do is keep them shiny. Kind of sad, isn't it, when we don't have anything better to do than polish shoes. Hey, look, here comes Lucy now." Bertha waved to the petite figure making her way across the hot pavement.

"Hi, everybody. The darndest thing just happened. Some kind of alarm clock kept going off in my apartment and I couldn't figure out where the noise was coming from. I opened every dresser drawer, rooted through the closet, opened kitchen drawers. Never did find the danged thing. It's weird."

For the first time Lucy seemed to be aware of the size of the group. "Why are you all standing out here in the broiling sun?"

"We're having a fire drill. Don't you remember? They announced yesterday that we would have a fire drill today at 2:30."

Lucy's face lit up and a smile split her round face. "THAT must have been the alarm sound I heard. It never occurred to me that it was a fire alarm."

"If it had gone off inside your apartment like it's supposed to, I guarantee you would never mistake it for a clock or timer. I hate the sound of that inside alarm, but even so I hope they get them repaired soon. I worry that we could all sleep through a major fire if we don't have alarms we can hear."

"Why, oh, why don't they sound the all-clear?" Glenna grumbled. "I wish I had put on something cooler this morning when I got dressed."

Mariana, current president of the Resident Association, spoke up. "That reminds me, at the town hall meeting the other day I wanted to bring up that we should talk about the dress code here at the Gardendale, but I decided that was not the time or place. I need to check the lease first and be sure that rule about not wearing shorts in the dining room is still in effect and whether it applies to both men and women. Have you noticed all these old guys coming to the dining room in shorts? And one of them doesn't wear any underwear!"

"Doesn't wear any underwear?" echoed Melba. "Who is it? And how in the world did you find out he doesn't wear any underwear?"

"It's Albert and let's just say I'm careful not to ever sit across from him anymore."

"Thanks for warning us," Melba laughed.

"Uh, oh, watch out, Bertha," cautioned Glenna. "You might want to be careful about leaning against that car. It's mine and it's filthy. I need to get it washed. It's a fairly new car, but I'm not very happy with it. There were several little things wrong with it so a couple of weeks ago I took it in to the shop to get it checked out and they supposedly fixed everything. Well, the rattle came back, so I took it back in a second time yesterday. I got treated like I was invisible. Do you know what I mean? Sometimes people ignore old people, especially old ladies, or treat them like they don't have the sense God gave a billy goat. The other day a young man on a bicycle yelled at me, 'Watch out, Grandma!' I had no intention of running over him, but after he yelled at me, I had an urge to chase him down and squash him. Well, anyway, at the auto shop I was being ignored, so I had one of my 'sophisticated snit fits.'"

"What in the world is a 'sophisticated snit fit?'" asked Bertha.

"That's what we called it when I was growing up in South Georgia. It's when you don't lower yourself to a trashy level, but you maintain your self-esteem and your knowledge and calmly and continually repeat what the problem is and how to fix it if you know how--and I did. So they finally listened and I have my car back--again. I guess in time I will know if it's fixed." She sighed. "Life's little complexities. Ah, at last, there's the all-clear. Let's get back to where it's cool."

Bertha and Melba were walking back through the Fountain Courtyard when Bertha nudged Melba with her elbow. "Good gosh, can you believe it? Audrey is sitting outside her apartment in this ninety-degree heat and of all things, she is knitting. Probably using wool yarn, too, just to up the heat level. Is the woman crazy?"

"Probably, a little. Or maybe her body thermostat is out of whack like that of so many old folks. But, ouch, it makes me even hotter just to look at her."

"Hi, Audrey," Bertha said as they approached

the busily knitting woman, her needles flying and clicking away in the hot sunlight. "Aren't you miserable doing that out here in this wretched heat?"

"No, not at all. You know how cold-natured I am. This feels good to me. And besides, I can see what I'm doing lot better out here than inside the apartment."

"What are you making?"

"This one here's a sweater."

"Yes, I see now. That must be one of the arms. Is it for somebody in your family?"

"Oh, no, they're for friends here at the Gardendale. By Christmas I should have a lot of them."

When Bertha and Melba were out of Audrey's earshot, Melba said, "You had better hope you're not on her Christmas list."

"Why?"

"Didn't you notice that sleeve she was working on? That thing dangled all the way to the ground and then some. Must be four feet long already."

"Oh, dear. Remember the sweaters Stella knitted for us? We didn't want to hurt her feelings so we all wore them. Same thing with Stella's sweaters--long, dangling sleeves. We tried rolling up those sleeves, pushing them up, even using rubber bands trying to keep them from hanging down, but the sweater sleeves always won the fight. Mine was major ugly, a sort of tomato soup color I hated."

"Oh, I remember. I wore mine once or twice, but you actually wore yours fairly often, didn't you?"

"Yep, sure did, until Stella died. Then I put it in the dog's bed. He loved it."

CHAPTER Six

Bertha plunked the carafe of coffee down on the table along with several little plastic tubs of coffee creamer.

"Bertha, why in the world don't you just wait and let Maricela bring our coffee? After all, that's her job." Sally turned her coffee cup right side up and moved it toward Bertha.

"Because I want my coffee as soon as I get to the breakfast table. I don't want to sit here every morning half asleep waiting for coffee." Bertha poured herself a cup and grabbed Sally's cup to fill. "So, any new gossip, Sally?"

"Not gossip, I guess, but there was lots of excitement last night on our courtyard. Admiral Raines caused another fire around 10:30. You know how he likes to cook late at night. Well, he was cooking himself some bacon and forgot about it.

The grease in the skillet caught fire and set off the smoke alarm. That brought the usual array of fire trucks and other emergency vehicles. No real damage done, but it sure makes us worry that he might burn down the whole complex."

"What that old coot needs is a wife," said Evie. "Wonder if there is anybody here who would marry him."

"Yeah," agreed Melba, "just having somebody else in that apartment with him might save all our lives someday. He has the biggest apartment in the complex and I understand he has pots of money, so we ought to be able to find somebody who will marry him."

"I don't know him very well," Sally said. "Does he have any eccentricities or bad habits that might scare a potential wife away?" No one answered.

Evie buttered her biscuit. "Did you know that he took me out to dinner several times when he was still driving?"

"Are you telling us you actually *dated* the Admiral?" Sally asked excitedly. "Wow, Evie, you have a secret life! What happened? Did you dump him or vice versa? Oh, this is juicy."

"I guess it was sort of a mutual dumping. The relationship died a natural death. Since then he has taken a shine to several ladies here, but nothing has come of it. Bertha, you haven't said anything. Do you know anything about the Admiral?"

"Well, I heard a story about him, but I shouldn't repeat it because I don't know for sure if it's true."

Melba swallowed her bite of toast. "Humph, after that little tidbit, you have to tell us the story, so you might as well go ahead."

Bertha took a sip of coffee. "Okay, here it is. A couple of months ago Janie went to the laundry room to get her clothes out of the dryer and the Admiral was in there loading a washing machine. Janie had begun folding and stacking her clothes in her laundry cart when she realized she didn't have her door keys with her. Well, you know how much they preach to us about keeping up with those keys whenever we leave our apartment. So she rushed back to her apartment and sure enough, there were her keys in the door. Janie grabbed her keys and went right back to the laundry room, but nobody was in there.

"Janie finished putting her clothes in her cart, but when she got back to her apartment and began to put her clothes away, she discovered that every pair of underpants she had put in the cart was gone. All she could figure out was that the Admiral had taken them."

"Good gosh, that's creepy." Sally scraped her cut-up fruit from its bowl into her take-home container. "Do we want to fix up anybody like that with a wife? I don't think so!"

"That behavior is a little eccentric," said Evie, "but remember, we don't know for sure that the Admiral took the underpants. Maybe somebody else popped in there and grabbed them. It could have happened that way."

Bertha suspected that Evie was more anxious than the rest of them to find a wife for the Admiral. After all, her apartment was only two units away from his and a fire might spread quickly to her place.

"I followed a purple lampshade the other day," Melba blurted out. "It had gold and purple beads hanging down from it."

"What?" asked Sally, trying to figure out what such a bizarre statement had to do with finding the Admiral a wife. "You followed a purple lampshade?"

"Sure did. A mover was carrying it down the corridor and I was curious to see who would own such a lampshade, so I followed him to an apartment on the front of the building. A new resident was moving in and would you believe, almost everything she owned was purple! Purple sofa and chairs, lavender rug, purple dishes. She was even wearing a purple beret. So I was thinking that if the Admiral is eccentric enough to steal underpants, he might like an eccentric lady friend."

"It wouldn't hurt to check her out," said Evie. "Do you think you could discreetly find out if she is interested in meeting a man?"

"That shouldn't be a problem. I'll let you know what I learn."

Melba reported back to the group in a few days. "It's no go with Inez (that's the purple lady's name.) Seems she already has a gentleman friend who lives with his children nearby and she moved to The Gardendale to be close to her boyfriend. So we need to find somebody else."

"I've been thinking about it and I've come up with an idea," said Sally. "I'm on the welcoming committee to greet new residents. We are supposed to make them feel at home here and one of the ways we do that is to find them a place to sit at lunch and breakfast."

"That is absolutely the best thing you can do for a new resident," interrupted Bertha, before Sally could finish. "I remember when I first moved in here and tried to find a place to sit: 'I'm sorry, that's Arabella's place,' or 'Arnold sits there,' or 'We don't have room at our table.' At one table somebody even said, 'Betty Ann is out of town for two weeks, but that's her seat and we can't let anyone sit there.'

"I suspected it would be that way--I've even seen that kind of behavior with church pews--but when I first moved in here, I felt like such an outcast that for three weeks I picked up my meals and ate in my apartment. So believe me, I am glad the welcoming committee is doing something about that problem. But you were about to tell us something, Sally. I'm sorry I interrupted."

At that moment Melba reached for one of the small coffee creamer tubs and held it up. "Did you know these little tubs make great trash cans for dollhouses?"

Evie punched Bertha and whispered, "Now, where in the world did *that* come from?"

Bertha whispered back. "Darned if I know. Sometimes she is just off in la la land."

Sally continued as though nothing had happened. "The Admiral is alone at his table at both meals since his friend Henry died and Lavelle moved away. So I am going to start steering any attractive prospects to his table and we'll see what develops. I'll give the Admiral a good build up, too, so he'll sound like the catch of the century."

"Go for it," said Evie. "And if you find somebody you think is interested in him, we might be able to do a little PR for him ourselves. We might get the old geezer married after all."

"Hmm," Bertha mused. "You have called him an 'old coot' and an 'old geezer.' One might assume your romance didn't go any too well."

"There wasn't any romance, and you are right, the relationship didn't go very well. Sally, I wish you well on your efforts to find him a mate."

CHAPTER Seven

A few days later Sally hurried to the lunch table.
"Hi, Sally," Evie said with a wave of her hand. "Where were you yesterday and this morning? We were worried about you."

"Oh, I had some errands," Sally answered vaguely and hurriedly changed the subject. "I've got the perfect candidate for the Admiral. Wait until you see her! She's attractive, wears a blond curly wig, her makeup is perfect, and she's dressed to the nines, unlike most of the population here. I'll bet she doesn't even own a sweatshirt. She's moving into her apartment today and I'll seat her at the Admiral's table in the morning.

"Oh, and she is from the South and get this, her name is Lucy Belle Montclair. Is that Southern, or what? I think she is perfect for the Admiral!"

The next morning Bertha, Melba, and Evie were

seated at their breakfast table earlier than usual, not wanting to miss Lucy Belle's appearance.

"Look!" Bertha motioned toward the main entrance to the dining hall. "Sally and Lucy Belle are just coming in the door."

"Dang!" said Evie, "I wish I could see better. I'll be glad when the doctor removes these dadgum cataracts. What does she look like?"

"Exactly like Sally described her. She's a little bit plumper than I expected, but maybe the Admiral likes his women curvaceous. Maybe you were too skinny for him, Evie."

They watched as Sally approached the Admiral's table, Lucy Belle in tow. The Admiral rose from his chair, his face beaming with pleasure. Sally felt invisible as the Admiral gazed at Lucy Belle with moonstruck eyes.

"Admiral, this is Lucy Belle Montclair. She just moved here from Atlanta to be closer to her children."

The Admiral quickly stepped over to pull out the chair next to his. "Hello, young lady, and welcome to The Gardendale."

Lucy Belle batted her eyelashes and smiled demurely. "Why, hello, Admiral. I am so delighted to meet you."

Still grinning broadly, the Admiral pushed Lucy Belle's chair in, then took his seat beside her.

"Enjoy your breakfast," Sally called, as she left their table and made her way to her friends.

"Oh, man," Sally said excitedly, sitting down and reaching for the coffee. "I think we have a winner. I could actually feel the chemistry." She wriggled with excitement. "This is so much fun."

"Should we be meddling like this in somebody else's life? There are some really nice men here so maybe we should let Lucy Belle do her own shopping for a boyfriend or husband."

"Bertha, don't fret so. If it's meant to be, it will all work out. If it's not, the relationship will fall apart.

*****

As the days went by, the friendship between Lucy Belle and the Admiral seemed to deepen. The two of them sat together at the weekly movies in the Community Center, went to exercise class together, and several times even went to a nearby restaurant for their evening meal.

"The romance with the Admiral and Lucy Belle is going even better than we expected," Bertha commented one day at lunch. "It's love in bloom! Last night I was out for my usual walk around the complex and I heard my favorite CD being played--you know, that Harry Allen jazz album of songs from the 1940's. Oh, that music is so romantic!" she sighed.

Her friends listened with full attention--nobody even took a bite.

"Well, I kept getting closer to the music and discovered it was coming from Lucy Belle's apartment. You know how proper she is--she believes you shouldn't entertain a gentleman in your apartment with the blinds closed. So of course I could see right in. And she and the Admiral were dancing--that wonderful slow dancing we used to do. I tell you, it looked so sweet and romantic that I nearly cried."

"It's working, girls, it's working," said Melba gleefully. "This makes me feel good all over."

"Yeah," said Evie, skepticism in her voice, "it seems too good to be true. Shouldn't the road to romance be a little more rocky than this?"

"Oh, Evie," said Melba, "don't burst the bubble. This place needs a good romance. It's full of people lonely for their deceased spouse and this business with the Admiral and Lucy Belle makes us all feel good."

A few days later at breakfast, the friends noticed that the Admiral was eating alone.

"I hope Lucy Belle isn't sick," Evie commented.

"No, she's okay," said Sally. "She went back to Atlanta for three weeks to visit her sister. I think her sister had some kind of surgery."

"Oh, dear. I hope the Admiral behaves himself while she's gone," said Evie.

"Honestly, Evie, you are such a skeptic," said Melba. "Why would you say such a thing?"

"I just think our hotshot Admiral has a roving eye, that's all."

"Well, I hope not," said Melba.

Sally chimed in. "I can see how you might feel that way. After George, it's hard not to be a little bit wary of all the old guys in this place. Do you remember George?"

"That must have been before I came here," said Evie. "Tell me about George."

"That lecherous old bozo couldn't keep his hands off the ladies. He was always putting his hands where they didn't belong. One day he came up behind me when I was at my mailbox and wrapped his arms around me. It startled me so much I reached my arm out and turned around and whacked him. To my surprise, I knocked him down to the floor! But that didn't stop him. He tried it again one day when I was leaving the dining room, so I hit him again and told him, 'Don't you EVER touch me again.'"

Bertha's mouth fell open. "You actually hit him both times?"

"Yes, I did. It was more of a protective reaction, really. I didn't mean to knock him down, but looking back on it, I'm glad I did."

"Does he still live here?"

"No, as a matter of fact, he was asked to leave, thank goodness. I have often wondered where he went."

"Maybe to a home full of lecherous old ladies," Melba giggled. "Oh, my, now there's a picture!"

"Well, surely the Admiral isn't as bad as old George was, or we would know it by now," Sally said. "I sure don't want Lucy Belle to have to put up with such shenanigans."

*****

Exactly two weeks later, Bertha slammed the coffee carafe down on the breakfast table. Her anger spilled out on the group like an overturned cup of scalding coffee. "I'm so mad at that darned Admiral. How did our government ever trust such a snake to command a ship?"

"I've never seen you so angry. What happened?" asked Sally.

"That stupid jerk of a man took another woman out to dinner last night. Sneaky devil. He took DeeDee--you know, the redhead who lives by the swimming pool--to the Chinese restaurant across the street. Apparently they arranged to meet at the restaurant. I guess he didn't want anybody seeing them walking over there together. But some of the residents were eating there and saw them sitting in a booth making eyes at each other."

"Maybe it was only a friendly supper, just that one time," said Melba.

"I wish, but I know he took her there at least one other time since Lucy Belle has been gone. Old philanderer. Poor Lucy Belle."

"She'll be back in a week and we'll just have to wait and see what happens then," said Evie. "Let's hope they take up where they left off and Lucy Belle never hears about that other gal."

*****

A week later, Evie rushed to the breakfast table where Sally and Bertha were already were sipping their coffee. "Have you heard what happened last night?"

"If you are talking about Lucy Belle and the

Admiral, yes, we heard. But it's hard to believe. She seems like such a sweet, mild-mannered Southern lady that I can't believe she did that."

"Who did what?" asked Melba coming up behind Evie, as usual a bit late for breakfast.

Sally answered. "Lucy Belle returned from her trip last night, one night earlier than expected. She put her luggage inside her apartment and then hurried to the Admiral's apartment to let him know she was home."

"Uh, oh, I know what's coming," said Melba, parking her walker, then settling herself in her chair. "DeeDee was there."

"Right. But wait until you hear what happened next! DeeDee left in a hurry and Lucy Belle started yelling at the Admiral. Adele lives next door to him and she could hear every word right through the wall!

"Lucy Belle called the Admiral a two-timing, unfaithful, womanizing, lecherous old tomcat, and a few other names which are not mentioned in polite company. And then she picked up the object nearest her which happened to be a picture of the Admiral's grandsons and threw that frame right at his head like a discus thrower."

Melba's eyes grew large. "Oh, my gosh. Did it hit him?"

"I'll say it hit him. It skidded across the side of his face and the sharp edge of that frame cut him all the way across his cheek. He bled like a stuck pig and scared the dickens out of Lucy Belle. She thought she had killed him. She called 911 and the EMS guys came and hauled him off to the hospital. He had to have fifteen stitches in that sorry head of his."

"So much for romance and getting the Admiral married," sighed Evie.

For the next couple of days, neither the Admiral nor Lucy Belle came to meals.

At lunch on the third day after the much-talked-about fight, the chatter of the residents suddenly stopped. The whole dining room grew quiet. The Admiral was walking to the center of the room, one side of his face swathed in a big bandage. Beside him was Lucy Belle. Both were beaming like children told they could eat all the chocolate they wanted. Alfred, the dining room manager, handed the Admiral a microphone.

"Is this thing on, Alfred?" asked the Admiral. Alfred nodded.

"Attention, everybody," the Admiral boomed out in a commanding voice. "I want to announce to all of you that the lovely Ms. Lucy Belle Montclair and I are getting married in three weeks. The wedding will be in the rose garden and you're all invited."

When the clapping died down, the Admiral continued. "Never thought I would find a new First Mate at my age," he boomed, "but Lucy Belle is my kind of woman: fiery temper, jealous as hell, and knows how to treat her man!"

Lucy Belle grabbed the microphone. "And the Admiral knows how to treat me," she burbled happily. "Just look at this." With that, she held up her left hand, which was adorned with a diamond that looked big enough to sink a ship.

The four matchmakers high-fived across the table. Sally beamed. "Are we good, or what?

The others answered in a chorus: "We are good!"

CHAPTER Eight

Evie stuck her head out of her apartment door and called to Sally, "I know you must be on your way to lunch, but could you come in here for just a minute? I have a problem."

Sally skirted the cleaning equipment outside to get to Evie's doorway. "What's the problem?"

"I can't seem to get across to Maria that she doesn't need to clean the stove every week. I don't use it that much and there's no need for her to spend time cleaning something that's already clean. I sure wish that somewhere along the line I had learned at least a little bit of Spanish."

"Yeah, it would be helpful here. Most of the housekeeping staff and dining room servers are Hispanic and in fact, I think they all knew each other back in El Salvador. Some of the residents here get mad because the girls aren't fluent in English, but let me tell you, I would have a tough time if suddenly I were working in El Salvador. Let me see what I can do."

Sally stepped into the apartment and walked into the kitchen. "Maria," she called.

Maria came out of the bathroom to the kitchen door. *"Si?"*

"Oh, boy. How do I do this?" Sally pointed to the stove. "Ummm, Maria, uh, let's see; okay, you no clean stove. Ugh, I sound like Tonto. That won't work. Let me think. Okay, *no limpie este,*" Sally said, pointing to the stove.

Maria grinned. *"Si, no debo limpiar la estufa. Gracias!"*

Evie padded to the door with Sally and stepped outside. "What did she say?"

"Beats me. I think she was saying she understands that you don't want the stove cleaned. You'll have to wait and see if we got the message across."

"I'm impressed, Sally. I didn't know you knew Spanish."

"Well, you just heard almost the whole extent of my Spanish vocabulary."

"Thanks for your help. I'll be in to lunch in a minute."

Her friends were already eating their soup when Evie sat down at the table. "Looks good," she commented. "What kind of soup is it?"

Melba answered, "It's chicken gumbo and it's wonderful. We must have a new cook here who's Cajun 'cause this tastes just like the gumbo my mama made when I was growing up in Louisiana. And look, the cornbread isn't falling apart anymore. Somebody's doing something different back there in the kitchen."

"I'll have the soup, too, please," Evie told one of the servers, pointing to her neighbor's bowl; she then turned her attention to her friends. "Did you gals know that Sally speaks Spanish? She helped me communicate with Maria today."

"No, Evie, I do not speak Spanish," Sally insisted. "I know only a few words, that's all, and I just happened to remember enough to help you tell Maria not to clean your stove. I didn't even know the word for stove. I had to point to it and call it 'this.'"

"I wish I knew even a few words of Spanish," said Bertha. "Well, I guess I do know one sentence. *Donde esta el bano?* But it would be nice to know enough to chat with our housekeeping staff sometime and not just be able to ask them where the bathroom is. I see Martha talking to them and I'm envious."

"Didn't Martha live for a while in Mexico?" asked Melba.

"Yes, for nearly 40 years, so of course she is fluent in Spanish."

The entrees arrived at the table and the women busied themselves passing gravy, buttering cornbread, cutting meat.

"I have an idea," said Melba. "Why don't we ask Martha if she would teach us some Spanish? We could have a little class once or twice a week and we could offer to pay although I doubt she'd take money for it."

"Melba, that's a great idea," replied Bertha. "Why don't we ask her as soon as lunch is over?"

"I'll call her," offered Sally, "and let you know tomorrow what she says."

At breakfast the next morning, Sally announced, "Martha was excited about our idea for a Spanish class. She said she would love to have more people, but there is only room for the four of us in her apartment. She also said that Monday and Wednesday afternoons at three work best for her. Does everybody want to go?"

"Sounds good," Evie said. "I'm in."

"Me, too," chorused Melba and Bertha.

"Okay, then. I'll tell Martha it's a deal and we'll plan to start Wednesday. By the way, I asked her about our paying her and she insisted we not do that. She said these lessons would give her a chance to use her Spanish and would be fun besides."

"Do we need to buy books or anything?" Melba asked.

"I asked Martha about that. She thinks she can persuade the office to print out our lesson sheets and we can each keep them in a notebook. You know Martha--she is very organized, so I'll bet these lessons will be really good and well worth keeping."

*****

"Good, you're early," Martha greeted the group

at her apartment door. "And you all got here at the same time. Good job. Come on in." When they were all seated, Martha handed each one a printed sheet of paper.

"I think that since the best opportunity for you to use your Spanish is with the servers in the dining room, we'll begin there. It will be more fun if you have a few actual questions and phrases you can use right away. Then if you are interested, later on we can get more into the rules for pronunciation and grammar.

"Let's say you are at breakfast and your coffee carafe is empty. You want to ask for more coffee, so you tell Maricela, *'Mas cafe, por favor.'* I'm sure you already know that *por favor* means please and you probably know that *cafe* is coffee, so that leaves *mas* which is of course more. *Mas cafe, por favor*. Okay, let's all say it together."

The friends repeated the phrase together, and then Martha had each one say it.

"Very good," said Martha, "you can now ask for more coffee in Spanish. You are going to find that the servers will give you some big smiles. Don't ever think they are laughing at your Spanish. They are always just plain delighted that someone is making the effort to learn their language. And, by the way, I have told them what we are doing and asked them to help you if there's an opportunity. Is that all right with you?" The four nodded.

CHAPTER Nine

As the days went by, the notebooks grew thicker with lesson sheets, many with scribbled notations on them. In the dining room the friends were getting bolder in using their Spanish and were feeling quite pleased with themselves.

"We're not exactly what I would call bilingual," commented Sally one morning, "but we are learning to communicate a little in Spanish and it's really fun."

"By the way," asked Bertha, "did you all read about the new exhibit at the museum? It's about the Hispanic culture and has a lot of arts and crafts from Mexico and Central and South America. Why don't we all go tomorrow morning? We'll probably appreciate the exhibit even more now that we are a little familiar with the language."

"Good idea," agreed Evie. "There was an interesting article about the exhibit in Sunday's paper with several photos."

"Do you all have your cemetery plots?" Melba suddenly asked. The group was silent for a moment, brains trying to connect Melba's remark with the current topic of conversation.

"Melba, why did you all of a sudden ask that?" queried Bertha, still trying to make the connection in her mind.

"Because I don't have anyplace to go when I die, so my son and I are going Friday to pick out a plot at Wesley Oaks Cemetery."

"That's nice, Melba," said Evie kindly. "I'm glad you are going on Friday because that means you can still go to the museum with us tomorrow."

"Oh, yes," said Melba, "I sure don't want to miss that exhibit."

Bertha felt thoroughly rattled by Melba's comments and had a hard time getting back on track. On the way back to their apartments, Bertha asked Evie, "Do you think Melba is okay? I'm concerned about her. She seems ditzier than ever."

"I think she's okay. I've been thinking about it and have decided it may have something to do with her hearing. She misses a lot of the conversation so is thinking about other things. It sure is disconcerting, though, when she pops up with stuff like that. Our cemetery plots, for goodness sake!"

"I hadn't thought about her hearing. Of course! That's got to be it. It's hard enough to keep up with our chitchat when you can hear all that's being said. I can see where you could easily lose out if you can't hear very well. You've made me feel better."

Several days later at lunch, Bertha turned to Melba who was seated next to her, "Melba, I was walking by your apartment this morning. Your door was open and I thought I heard you talking to yourself."

"I was practicing my Spanish that time, but I talk to myself all the time."

"You do? Does that worry you?"

"Of course not, why should it? Who else is there to talk to? I'm a good listener and have plenty of time to listen to myself. Once in a while I get bored with what I have to say, but most of the time I'm okay with it. I understand what I mean without having to explain it. And you should appreciate this--it saves my friends from having to listen to all that stuff!"

Melba continued. "That reminds me of something--a quotation I memorized after my husband died when I felt lonelier than I have ever felt in my entire life.

"Seneca wrote this way back in 4 B.C., 'Listen to me for a day, for an hour, a moment, lest I expire in my terrible wilderness, my lonely silence. Oh, God, is there no one to listen?'

"So, see? I have solved the problem! I'm always there for me to talk to!"

Everyone at the table sat silently, suddenly contemplative.

As Bertha and Sally left the dining room together, Bertha said, "What a remarkable conversation! I never thought anything Melba says would ever make much sense to me, but there's a convoluted brilliance to the things she said today--certainly food for thought."

"Yeah, it really makes you wonder what she was like in her younger days. Did you know she once taught English in a college in her home town?"

"I didn't know that, but now that I think about it, sometimes I see glimpses of that."

*****

After one of their Spanish lessons, Melba asked, "Have you noticed how many Spanish words sound like our English words except that they just stick an 'o' on the end? Like our word, bank--they say *banco*. Of course you add an 'a' if it's a feminine word," she declared somewhat smugly. "And if it's plural, you just add an 's' onto the end of that-- *bancos*. Couldn't be simpler!"

Melba continued. "All this talk about Spanish gives me an idea. This evening why don't we walk down the street to El Loro Verde and have supper there? I'm hungry for Mexican food and we can practice our Spanish because almost everybody who works there is Hispanic. Let's meet at the front desk downstairs about six and walk to the restaurant together."

"Super idea," Bertha said, and the others agreed.

The four friends met in the lobby at six and a few minutes later were seated at a booth in the colorfully decorated restaurant. Their server brought a basket of hot chips and two bowls of salsa. "Yum," said Sally, dipping a chip into the thick red sauce.

They gave their orders and settled down to enjoy their appetizer while they waited.

"Sometimes I like to sprinkle the hot chips with a little salt," said Melba, reaching across the table for the saltshaker. As she did so, she knocked over her glass of water. Everyone scrambled to mop up the puddles of water and in the confusion, Sally knocked over her full glass, sending another stream of water over the table and down into her lap.

The busboy rushed over with several big cloth napkins and for a few minutes everyone concentrated on cleaning up the mess.

Mopping furiously, Melba said to the busboy, "Sorry to make such a mess. We are so embarrassed."

At his puzzled look, she decided to try her Spanish. *"Estamos embarazadas,"* she chirped.

The busboy looked stunned.

"Que?" he stuttered. *"Embarazadas? Ustedes?"*

"Si," Melba continued, pleased with her success.

"Todas ustedes?"

"Si, estamos embarazadas todas."

With that, the busboy grabbed all the napkins and hurried to the kitchen. Moments later, he and several of the waiters were in the kitchen doorway.

"Don't look now," said Bertha, "but the busboy is standing at the door to the kitchen with some of the waiters and they are laughing. One of them is pointing to us. I don't think those grins are the 'delighted smiles' Martha was talking about. What in the world did you say to him, Melba?"

"Well, nothing much. You heard it all. I told him

we were all embarrassed. Weren't you embarrassed at the big mess we made? All I said was '*Estamos embarazadas*'—'We are embarrassed.' And then he asked if all of us were embarrassed and I said, yes, we are all embarrassed. I thought I did rather well with my Spanish so I can't imagine what is so funny."

The four friends ambled back to the complex still puzzling over what Melba could have said that was so amusing. As they entered the front of the building, Sally said, "Look! Consuela is at the desk tonight. Let's ask her about what Melba said and maybe she can enlighten us.

"Hi, Consuela. We're just coming back from dinner at El Loro Verde and need to ask you something." Turning to Melba, Sally said, "Melba, tell Consuela exactly what you told the fellow in the restaurant."

Melba carefully recited her exact words to the busboy.

Consuela tried to keep a straight face as she asked, "Those were your exact words?"

"Yes, why? What is so funny about telling him we were embarrassed?"

"Because you didn't tell him you were embarrassed; you told him you were all PREGNANT!"

"Oh, Melba, no wonder they laughed," said Evie. "Four white-haired old ladies insisting they are pregnant. That is just too funny!"

Consuela joined in as they laughed until their sides hurt. Finally Melba admitted, "I guess there is a little more to Spanish than just adding another letter to the end of a word."

CHAPTER Ten

"Where is Sally?" Evie asked Bertha as she draped her sweater over the back of the chair beside Bertha.

"She came to the dining room early and if you look across the room way over in the corner, you'll see her sitting with Raymond and Irma."

"I can't see that far," said Evie. "Danged cataracts. Can you see her, Melba?"

"Yep, sure can. She's talking away to Raymond. But why is she sitting over there and not with us?"

Bertha shook her head and rolled her eyes. "She's mad at me."

"Mad at you? So mad she won't even sit with us? For goodness sake, why?"

"Do you really want to hear the whole story?"

"Of course we do," said Evie.

"Saturday she and I were chatting by the mailboxes when Olivia popped up beside me. Olivia waited politely, then asked me for the directions to my hairdresser, you know, the new lady I am going to. I really like the way she cuts my hair. With this haircut I don't even have to have a perm and you know how I hate perms because they always leave my hair kinky curly and I can't do a thing with my hair when I have one of those kinky perms. It makes my hair look like a bale of barbed wire. Oh, dear, I got off track. What were we talking about?"

"You were telling us why Sally is mad at you," Melba answered.

"Oh, that's right. Olivia asked me for the driving directions to the beauty shop and I told her to go out of the entrance of The Gardendale, turn right on Cascade, go down the street two blocks, turn left on Lambert and she would see the beauty shop on her right."

Melba and Evie waited, then Evie said, "I don't understand. That's what made Sally mad?"

"Yes. When Olivia thanked me and left, Sally said, 'Those directions aren't right,' and I said, 'Of course, they are right. What's wrong with them?'

"Then she said, 'You'll have Olivia all mixed up because when you go out of the entrance of The Gardendale, if you turn right, you go UP the street, not DOWN the street. DOWN the street is the other way.'

"Then I said, 'Not to me, it isn't. Down the street is to the right and up the street is to the left.'

"Then she said, 'Oh, you are so wrong. Anybody knows if you turn right on Cascade you go UP the street.'

"About that time I felt my anger genes kicking in and I guess I raised my voice. 'For crying out loud what difference does it make? To you it's UP the street, to me it's DOWN the street. Everybody here knows where Lambert Street is anyway, so up or down, what earthly difference does it make?'

"And she said, 'Well, it certainly DOES make a difference if you don't know UP the street from DOWN the street when it is so obvious to the rest of us.' And she huffed off to her apartment and hasn't spoken to me since."

"Hmm," Melba said, "that's something I sure never thought about, up the street or down the street."

Bertha continued, "I hate to take anything that petty seriously, but she did make me curious, so I researched it when I got back to my apartment. I couldn't find a clue. Apparently, it doesn't matter one iota which one you call it. I suppose if the street were on a hill, she might have a point, but as flat as this city is, it seems absurd to get so bent out of shape over 'up the street' or 'down the street.'"

"This doesn't sound like Sally at all," said Evie. "She's been a little testy with all of us lately. Something must be wrong." Evie looked Bertha in the eye. "Well?" she questioned.

"Well, what?"

"Well, are you going to feud forever like the Hatfields and McCoys or are you going to do something about it and stop this foolishness? You need to get things back on an even keel, especially if Sally has a problem."

Bertha sighed deeply. "You're right. I guess I'll do something about it. Sally is more stubborn than I am so I suppose it's up to me to make the first move. I'll go by her apartment this afternoon."

Later that day Bertha locked her front door and headed over to Sally's apartment. She tapped the knocker gently, almost hoping Sally wasn't home, but in a moment Sally opened the door.

"Oh, hello, Bertha," Sally said, dispiritedly, as she stood with her hand on the doorknob.

"Well, may I come in?"

"Oh, okay, come on in. Have a seat. Want a cup of tea or coffee?"

"No, thanks. I'm still full of lunch. Sally, I'm sure you can guess why I'm here. It's about that silly 'up the street'--'down the street' thing. We shouldn't let something that petty ruin our friendship."

"You're right, except to me it's not petty and I am quite sure I'm right and I didn't like the way you spoke to me."

"I do apologize for speaking so harshly. Say, I have a suggestion. Since Melba was once a college English teacher, let's ask her about it. If she says you're right, I'll shut up and never mention it again. And if she says I'm right....well, I'll shut up and never mention it again! What do you think?"

"Okay, I'll go along with that. But I'm positive Melba will agree with me. Why don't I call her right now and see if we can go to her place and get this thing settled?"

A few minutes later, the two were at Melba's

door. "Come on in," she called, "the door's unlocked and the peppermint tea is brewing."

As soon as they were settled with their tea, Sally explained the situation to Melba, trying to present it fairly. Melba thought a minute, then pronounced solemnly, "Here is my judgment in the case."

Sally and Bertha waited.

"Whole thing doesn't amount to a hill of beans. Not a dab of difference in 'up the street' and 'down the street.' It's just a matter of perception and you two each perceive it differently and I hope to great goodness this settles it and you two young people will quit acting so childish!" And she took a sip of her tea.

Sally giggled. "Well, I guess we got told, good and proper. I accept your verdict."

"So do I," said Bertha, with a smile. "So that's that. Thank you, Melba."

Melba was quiet for a moment, then said, "This takes me back to my teaching days, especially when I was teaching high school English before I got my Master's. I graded an awful lot of English papers in those days and "awful lot" was a good description of many of them. I wish I had kept more of them because they were so funny.

"I gave the students vocabulary words to put in sentences and I'll share a couple with you. One of the words was "peripatetic" which as you may know means 'walking about' or 'itinerant.' Why the English department ever required the kids to know that word is anybody's guess, but we had to teach it.

"Anyway, one student's sentence was 'His wife

told him not to peripatetic on the rug.'

"Another word was 'abridged' and this kid wrote, 'My dog had abridged legs.' You can see where both of these students were coming from, but they were just off track enough to make it funny.

"Oh, and here are two of my favorites. The class was asked to use "congenital" in a sentence. One student wrote 'The professor said his congenitals were showing all the time,' and another kid wrote 'He thought he was congenital, but his psychologist said he was ordinary.' I love that one!"

Melba was on a roll. "Oh, and I've got to share these with you," she said, pulling out a worn notebook from a drawer. "I saved some of my favorites. How about this one? 'Jefferson was 14 when his father died at the age of 9.'

"And check out the creative spelling in this next one. You can see that I began correcting it by underlining the misspelled words.

"'Dolly Madison was the third child of <u>Quacker</u> parents. She had two sons, one named John and the other one died like his father of the yellow fever <u>epidermic</u>. Senator Aaron Burr introduced the young <u>window</u> to James Madison.'

"And here's another one: 'Thurber went to the <u>pubic</u> school in Ohio.' Bet he got a good education there!"

She looked through the notebook. "Here's a good one, a definition of superficial: 'One who ficializes at the football game.'"

Melba chuckled. "Only a few more, I promise

you. One student's paper was entitled, 'Paul's Reverse Ride.' Bet you never knew Mr. Revere made his famous ride backwards.

"How about this one? The vocabulary word was 'allay' and the sentence using the word is "My grandmother allays in her grave."

"Okay, I have tortured you enough with tortured English, but I am going to give you a homework assignment." She handed each of them a piece of paper with one paragraph written on it.

"This short composition is so full of eloquent phrases and wonderful vocabulary words that I made several copies of it and just came across them recently. Your assignment is to tell me tomorrow at breakfast just what this student was saying."

Sally and Bertha took the papers and stood up to leave. "Melba, this has been an absolute treat. I can't believe all these things you have shared with us are for real, though."

"Trust me, Bertha, they are," Melba said. "See you tomorrow," she called as she closed the door behind her friends.

"That was fun," said Sally. "Our little disagreement seems sillier than ever, don't you think?"

"For sure," Bertha agreed. "Well, let's go home and do our homework." She smiled. "It was fun seeing Melba in her 'teacher mode.' See you tomorrow."

Sally entered her apartment and sat down in her favorite chair. She switched on the lamp beside her. Written on the paper in a neat hand were the following words:

Paragraph Developed by Exposition

Due to the prerequisites that were enumerated for my degree in political science made me feel always impressive of the hard work which went along. Following many hours of reflection, my result was that having capable of completing the work which was recommended, elaborated persistency revealed much of the matter. Since all of my days of school which kept on comtemplating through my head, especially to where a noticeable eye can be seen on me working away for my accomplishment of the real truth. Extremely the preceding still lingered on. Before decisively as time passed, all the pieces soon came together.

Sally read the paragraph again and then a third time. Wow, she thought to herself, grading papers like this must have been a real challenge.

At breakfast, Melba asked Sally and Bertha if they could tell her in a sentence or two what the student was saying in the short composition.

Shaking her head, Sally said, "It made me feel really fuzzy-brained. It sort of made sense, but not exactly. I read it about four times, but I don't think I can tell you what it means."

"Same thing with me," said Bertha. "You know, that paragraph is fascinating. It seems so heartfelt and sincere, and the student's words are just pouring out onto the paper. He ended it by saying, 'Before decisively as time passed, all the pieces came together.' but the pieces never quite came together for me."

"Melba, I'm sure Sally agrees with me that we have new respect for you. From now on, I'm seeing our English language in a whole new light, thanks to you."

CHAPTER Eleven

"Well, you sure look droopy and down today. What in the world's the matter?" Bertha asked as she slid her chair over to make room for Evie at the table.

"You're right, I am down. I just feel sad," Evie replied. "I've had a triple dose of bad news already today. First of all, another apartment was burgled last night. It was the same as the other burglaries with no sign of anybody breaking in and nothing big taken, no electronics or TVs or anything. Apparently the burglar just grabbed a bunch of jewelry."

"Hmmm," said Sally. "As far as I know, we're the only burglars around here and we sure aren't stealing these things from people's apartments. It's really creepy to know that somebody can get into our apartment so easily. What other bad news did you get, Evie?"

"Well, it seems that Ruth--the Ruth who lives on the third floor near you, Bertha,--anyway, it seems that Ruth got hit this morning by the Houston Daily News and ended up in the hospital with a concussion."

"Wait a minute," said Sally. "Surely you didn't just say what I think you said. Ruth has a concussion because she got hit in the head with a newspaper?"

"Well, yes, in a manner of speaking. Have you ever watched the way our carrier throws the papers? He never comes up onto the second or third floor. He just stands at the bottom of the building and slings the papers up onto the balconies. Wham! The paper often wakes me up at 4:30 in the morning when he delivers it.

"I watched him one morning. You know how heavy the Sunday paper is. Well, he grabbed hold of that fat plastic bag stuffed with rolled up newspaper, swung it between his legs and then let fly, right up over the balcony railing and slam, into the apartment wall.

"One Sunday morning I couldn't sleep so I got up when I heard the papers slamming against the apartments. I opened the door expecting to see the paper outside, but it wasn't there so I stuck my head out the door to look up and down the balcony. Right then my paper hit the doorframe just inches from my head and I know it would have knocked me over if it had hit me. Scared the bejeebers out of me.

"Anyway, back to Ruth. She had done the same thing I did, but that heavy Sunday paper actually hit her. It knocked her backward and she stumbled and fell. She hit the back of her head against a console on the side wall near the door, and it gave her a concussion."

"Poor Ruth," said Bertha. "She has enough problems what with her diabetes and bad heart. That's just a shame. But you said three bad things happened. What is the other one?"

"This is the other one. Do you remember Nanette who was my neighbor when I lived on the other side of the complex? No, I guess you wouldn't remember her because she is so reclusive nobody knows her. She stays in her apartment and even picks up her meals in the dining room and takes them to her apartment where she eats them all alone. I don't think she has a friend in this whole place. And now things have gotten even worse."

"Worse, how?" asked Bertha.

"Just generally worse. I still try to go by and check on her several times a week and I'm worried about her. She's gradually letting herself go. She doesn't bother to put her teeth in, she doesn't wash or comb her hair. Poor thing. She tries to put makeup on and ends up with lipstick smeared on crooked and rouge spread all over her face. I guess she thinks it's powder."

"My gosh," exclaimed Sally. "Sounds like she's ready to move somewhere else to another level of care. What about her children? Does she have any?"

"Yeah, she has a son. I got so concerned about her that I went to the counselor to see if something could be done, like maybe getting her a caregiver or even moving her to another facility with a higher level of care, like you suggested. I told Margo all about how Nanette forgets that the dining room isn't open on weekends and evenings. She goes to pick up her food and everything is shut down and she is furious because nobody told her the dining room would be closed. Margo said she would look into the situation.

"I also talked with somebody else on the staff here, in fact, somebody higher up on the ladder than Margo. This person is sort of my 'secret source.' I call her my secret source because she tells me stuff she shouldn't be telling anybody and I wouldn't want to get her in trouble. Anyway, she says that Eddie, Nanette's son, denies there is anything wrong with his mother. He says that sometimes she just gets a little addled because of medication she is taking and he insists that she's just fine. He says she doesn't need any help or anything else.

"Also he was in the office trying to find out who is saying such things about his mother. They told him only that some of her neighbors were concerned. And he said, 'I'll bet it's that woman next door.'

"So one day somebody knocked on my door and I opened it and there he stood, looking like thunder. He'd even gone to the trouble of finding the new apartment I moved to. He glared at me and said, 'Look, you meddling old biddy, stay out of my mother's business. She's just fine and doesn't need you meddlesome old crows messing around in her life. I even heard you are trying to get her moved.'

"He glared at me and went on, 'Now you listen to me and you listen good. My mother is staying right where she is, she's just fine, and if you have any more contact with her, you are going to find yourself in big trouble. *You* just may be the one moving.' Then he stomped off back toward Nanette's apartment.

"I stood there at my door, stunned, and then the tears started. No one in my whole life has ever talked to me like that.

"I've tried a couple of times since then to talk to him and he just grunts at me and stomps off. Julie, one of the housekeepers, said that she knows Eddie and that he takes real good care of his mother. He does bring her food and sometimes even takes her out for lunch. But if I try to get her to go anywhere on the campus here, she seems afraid and always says, 'I can't go anywhere right now. I'm expecting my son to come any minute.' Bless her heart. I just don't know how to help her."

"One day," said Bertha, "when I was out taking a walk, I passed her apartment. The door was open, but I didn't see her anywhere around. I did catch a glimpse inside and there was a big portrait hanging over her sofa. It was a painting of a really knockout gorgeous woman. That wasn't a picture of Nanette, was it?"

"Yes, it is her portrait and you are right, she was beautiful when she was younger. And here's something else I'll bet will surprise you. She used to sing with a famous big band."

"Wow! Which band?" asked Sally.

"I don't know. She has forgotten, but she showed me stacks of music she has kept and once I even persuaded her to sing for me. Her voice was hardly even quivery and I guess you would describe it as sultry. I'll bet she was really something when she was younger. I feel so sorry for her now, just sort of unhappily drifting toward the end of her time here on earth."

Melba had been quiet, but she spoke up, her eyes dancing with what her friends called "that look." "Well, girls, we have our next project!"

"Yes!" Evie almost shouted. "We'll do a makeover just like they do on TV. Oh, oh, and we can even have a real pro to help us. My granddaughter is in town for a visit--you remember Stephanie. She's the one who studied in London to be a makeup artist and she's here for a month before she starts her new job in Chicago. Did I tell you she'll be working for a plastic surgeon doing makeup on disfigured people? I am so proud of her. Oh, my gosh, the timing is so perfect! Let's get started on our Nanette project right away."

"Whoa, slow down," Bertha cautioned. "You are getting me excited, too, but let's be practical. Even if Nanette consents, what about that son of hers? If he's such a horse's behind, he's not likely to want four meddling old women messing in his mother's life."

"Why does he have to know?" rejoined Evie. "He hardly ever comes to see her anyway and never in the middle of the week. And if he happens to find her looking better, then he'll just think she's feeling like her old self again. Maybe we'll get lucky and she'll forget to tell him about us."

Sally had a worried frown on her face. "I have a strong feeling that we shouldn't be jumping into the middle of this. It simply isn't any of our business."

Melba interjected, "But everything we do has a happy ending. I love happy endings."

"Melba," said Sally, "we have been lucky so far that everything has turned out all right. You are such a romantic, but you've got to remember--real life doesn't turn out like that."

"What do you mean? This IS real life!"

"What I mean is that we should quit while we're ahead and stop meddling before we mess somebody up."

"Okay, then," Melba shot back, "from now on we'll just sit back and enjoy things and let everybody's life get all fouled up and horrible while we just watch. You really think we should just sit on the sidelines and let that happen? I don't think so. What do you think God put us here for anyway?"

"I don't know," answered Sally. "I've been trying to figure that one out for a long time. I don't know why we are here. So many people we love are gone from us. Most of us feel like we should have been taken, too."

"Well, then," said Melba, "I guess there's some reason God left us here and if helping people isn't it, well, too bad."

"Okay, let's do it," said Sally resignedly. "But how do we do it? That's the big question. Sounds like we need to proceed gently and not overwhelm her."

Evie suggested, "How about if just Stephanie and I go the first time to visit and they can get acquainted?"

"Good idea," said Melba. "You can take Nanette some of my homemade cookies. And if she and Stephanie hit it off, that will give us a good start on our makeover. Then if Nanette seems to enjoy your visit, gradually all of us can drop in on her just to say hello or check on her."

"I'll go by Nanette's to set up a time with her," said Evie. "Let's see. Today is Friday. I'll wait until Monday so I won't run into Eddie in case he decides to come to see his mom this weekend."

Real life doesn't turn out like that. Sally thought about her comment to Melba and wondered again if she should confide in her friends. No, not until I know more, she decided.

CHAPTER Twelve

On Tuesday of the next week, Evie reported. "It's all set with Nanette for Thursday. Stephanie is as excited as we are and she's got a whole month available to help us."

Thursday afternoon Evie and Stephanie stood at Nanette's door with a plate of homemade chocolate chip cookies. "Stephanie, don't be surprised if Nanette has completely forgotten that we were coming today. She seems to be addled most of the time. Also, even though I lived next door to her for two years, I don't think she knows my name 'til yet—always calls me 'darling' or 'honey.'"

Evie lifted the brass knocker and let it drop several times. They could hear the TV inside, but no one came to the door. Evie knocked again, this time banging the knocker hard against its brass plate. The door opened a crack and Nanette peered out.

"Hi, honey," Nanette greeted Evie, her voice sounding faint against the loudness of the TV. She opened the door wider and moved to switch off the television.

"Come on in. I apologize for my appearance, but I wasn't expecting company." Nanette brushed unseen crumbs from the soiled pink blouse she wore over wrinkled gray pants. Her white hair hung in limp strands to her shoulders and sure enough, she had not put in her teeth. She had not bothered with any attempt at makeup and in Evie's eyes she just looked a sad mess.

"We brought you some homemade cookies. Nanette, this is my granddaughter, Stephanie. You might remember seeing her come to visit me when I lived next door to you."

"So that's where I know you from," Nanette responded to Evie. "I thought you looked familiar. And I think I remember this girl." She moved some magazines from the sofa. "Sit here. This sofa is real comfortable."

Evie hadn't given a thought to what they would talk about so she asked Nanette how she had been getting along.

"Oh, fine, I guess." Nanette attempted to smooth her wrinkled slacks. "You know, I should have been better dressed because my son will probably be here soon." Nanette reached for a cookie, while Evie gave a negative shake of her head to Stephanie.

"We won't plan to stay long, then, since Eddie may be coming. I just wanted Stephanie to meet you because I've been telling her about your career as a singer. Isn't this a portrait of you back then?" Evie asked, indicating the framed painting behind them over the sofa.

Nanette's eyes brightened. "Yes, that's me a long, long time ago. And how did you know I was a singer? Who told you that? It's true, of course. In fact, I have some of my sheet music right here."

Nanette opened the door to a small cabinet beside the sofa and pulled out a stack of music. "These are some of the songs I used to sing."

Evie and Stephanie leafed through the sheets of music. "Oh, look, here's 'Whispering'," exclaimed Evie. "That was always one of my favorites. And here's 'Memories.' These songs do bring back happy memories. Oh, and look! Here's a real oldie I loved and had almost forgotten about, 'So Glad I Found You.' Some of these go back even earlier than the 1940's."

"Yes, our band leader liked some of the earlier songs. He said they were great for dancing and I agreed. We usually did the newer songs for the college appearances and saved the older ones for those clubs which attracted an older crowd. I enjoyed singing all of them."

"Do you still sing any of these?"

"Only once in a while and of course only when I'm here alone." Nanette sighed. "My voice isn't what it used to be, that's for sure."

"I really would like to know more about what your life was like then," Stephanie said. "Did you travel with a band? And did you wear elegant and glamorous gowns?"

"I did travel some with one of the big bands. It was tiring and wonderful at the same time. I wish I could tell you the name of the band, but that's one of the things I have forgotten. Unbelievable, isn't it, that I would forget a thing like that? Anyway, we played for dances at lots of the big universities and at clubs around the country. This was in the late 1940's. I felt like a movie star holding that microphone and singing with the whole huge orchestra behind me. And everybody applauding after each number." Nanette's eyes sparkled as though she were reliving some of those moments.

"I wish you could have seen some of my dresses. They were designed especially for me and, oh, how beautiful they were." She sat quietly for a moment, then rose slowly from her chair. "I do believe I still have one of those dresses. I think I kept my favorite one. Sweetie," she said, addressing Stephanie, "if you'll come with me to the bedroom, I'll get you to pull a box from under my bed and we'll see if I really did keep that dress." Stephanie followed her into the bedroom and knelt beside the bed.

"Look for a big pale blue box," Nanette directed. "Do you see it?"

"Yes. Here it is." Stephanie pulled out the box and put it on top of the bed. Nanette called to Evie, "Honey, come on in here. We've found the box and if I'm right, the dress is inside."

When Evie got to the bed, Nanette removed the lid of the box to reveal something wrapped in layers of white tissue. "That's acid-free tissue," Nanette explained. "It's supposed to help keep the dress looking new." She folded back the tissue and pulled the cranberry red satin garment from its depths.

Stephanie gasped. "Oh, my gosh. That is absolutely gorgeous. I never saw anything like it. Look at the top part of it all covered with sequins and rhinestones. You must have looked like a queen in that."

"I sure did feel like a queen in it. I loved that dress--still do."

"Does it still fit you? Why don't you try it on for us?" Stephanie urged. "Please," she entreated.

"All right, I will. I am curious to see if it still fits me. You'll have to help me get it on," Nanette said, as she began to pull off her outer garments. Stephanie helped her slide the gown over her body and then zipped it up the back for her.

"It's a perfect fit. Wow, I'm impressed," she said.

Nanette preened and twirled in the dress. Then she bounced over to the full-length mirror and stared at her image. Tears began pouring down her cheeks. "It's still a wonderful dress--but I'm so ugly now, old and wrinkled and dirty and ugly." She turned to Stephanie. "Unzip this thing and put it back under the bed. I never want to look at it again." She grabbed a tissue and sobbed into it, then, still sniffling, she put her blouse and slacks back on.

Stephanie returned the dress to its box, then placed the box back under the bed. They walked back into the living room.

Stephanie put her arms around Nanette who was trying to stop crying, but with little success. "You know that beautiful young woman in the portrait over the sofa? You are right that you will never be that woman again. But do you realize what you still have?" Stephanie cupped Nanette's face in her hands. "You have terrific bone structure with wonderful high cheekbones. Yes, you have some wrinkles, but you obviously did not have a love affair with the sun because you sure don't have a lot of wrinkles. Now what else were you moaning about? Oh, yes 'ugly' and 'dirty.' Ugly you are not, trust me on that, and dirty--well, the particular clothes you have on are a little soiled, but a trip to the washing machine will solve that. So, see, no problems!"

Stephanie continued, one arm still around Nanette. "Tell you what. I've had such a good time visiting with you today, I want to come back. And if you'll let me come back to visit you, I'll show you some magic you won't believe. We will have such fun! How about next Tuesday?"

Nanette smiled. "Sweetie, will you really come back to see me? I would like that so much."

"You can count on it. Don't forget--next Tuesday, let's say about 2:30 in the afternoon."

Stephanie joined her grandmother and her friends for lunch the next day. Evie explained to them that she felt Stephanie and Nanette seemed to form a genuine bond during the short visit.

"And I'm going back next Tuesday," Stephanie said excitedly. "I called Jennifer, a friend of mine who's a hairdresser, to see if she could go with me and luckily it's her day off. She's going to cut and style Nanette's hair while I do her makeup. Then you are all invited to come by Nanette's for a visit. I think she is going to want to show off her new self. Oh, and if everything works out like I am planning, we'll have a big surprise for you. So be sure and save Tuesday afternoon. We'll probably be through and ready by four. I'll call you when we're ready."

CHAPTER Thirteen

Tuesday afternoon the four friends were together in Evie's apartment waiting for Stephanie's phone call. Evie spoke.

"Do you realize we have known each other for four years now? Odd, isn't it, that we all moved in about the same time and became such good friends so quickly?"

Evie, Bertha, Sally, and Melba had never met before moving into The Gardendale and they often discussed how quickly they had bonded and how firm that bond between them was. Each of them was widowed, but more important than that was the fact that each had lost a child to death. Two of them had lost children who were in their twenties and the other two had children who had died when they were in the early grades of school. As one of them once commented, "We all belong to a club that nobody wants to be a member of."

The friends had fought their way through these and other tragedies and had come out stronger for it. But they still had their "bad days" and could comfort and empathize with each other. They had shared tears and laughter and joys. And now they looked forward to the visit to Nanette and what they hoped would be a joy to share.

Finally the phone rang and Stephanie told them the time had come.

When they knocked on Nanette's door, Stephanie opened it and told them that Nanette was almost ready and motioned them to their seats. The chairs had been moved to face the same direction as the sofa.

When they were all seated, Stephanie's friend Jennifer stepped through the bedroom doorway and with a flourish, said, "May I present our star of the evening, the famed and incredible Nanette!"

Through the door stepped one of the most elegant women the friends had ever beheld! Nanette was a knockout. Jennifer had styled her silvery hair so that it swept to one side in a smooth pageboy and Stephanie had added makeup so subtle that you really didn't notice the makeup, just the beautiful skin, eyes, and glow.

And best of all, Nanette was dressed in the red dress.

"Oh, my gosh, Nanette," exclaimed Evie. "You look like you should step up and receive an Academy Award. You look fantastic!"

"But that's not all," said Stephanie. "We have

another surprise for you. I borrowed a friend's karaoke machine, found some discs of songs from the 40's and Nanette is going to sing for you." She handed Nanette a microphone.

The introduction to "So Glad I Found You" sounded from the machine, then Nanette began to sing. She was transformed. She was stunning. She was in performer mode and unstoppable. When she had finished the song, not missing a note or forgetting a single word, the four visitors stood and applauded and cheered while Nanette beamed and bowed and thanked them.

The friends left Jennifer and Stephanie with Nanette and made their way to The Gardendale's cozy library. They were too excited to go back to their apartments; they wanted to talk over the miracle they had just seen.

"Who would have believed it?" said Bertha. "That was amazing. She not only looked out-of-this-world gorgeous, but she really sang like a pro. And did she ever look happy!"

"Wow," agreed Sally, "it was amazing all right. And I hate to be the one to burst the bubble, but what do we do now? We've played Cinderella with Nanette and we can't just dump her now."

"You are sure right about that," Melba said. "We have meddled our way into the middle of this so let's just keep on meddling. Here's my idea. Do y'all know Delta Alexander, the woman who recently moved in across the courtyard from Nanette?"

"Aha," said Evie, nodding in agreement, "bet I

know what you're thinking. Tell us more."

"Okay, here's the deal. When Delta was introduced to us that first day she moved in, we were told that she plays the piano and used to be a lounge singer. So, obviously, we get the two of them together and see what happens. I don't know Delta at all, but I have a feeling that she would like to be a participant in this plot to rescue Nanette."

Melba suggested she herself be the one to talk to Delta, so she phoned Delta the next morning.

"Give me about fifteen minutes," Delta said, "then come on over."

Delta greeted Melba at the door. "Come on in and have a seat. I just made fresh coffee and some muffins. I have this recipe called 'Six-weeks Muffins.' You make the batter and it keeps in the fridge for six weeks. You just bake up a few whenever you want them."

"They sure smell good," Melba said. Delta moved aside some magazines on the coffee table, then set down a tray holding muffins on a plate beside two cups of steaming coffee. Melba took a bite of muffin. "These are delicious. Do you share recipes?"

"I can do better than that," Delta laughed. She got up and went to a bookshelf. She handed Melba a slim spiral-bound volume. "This is a little cookbook I wrote and the recipe for the muffins is in there along with a bunch of my other favorite recipes. Cook up some of them when you're in the mood and let me know what you think."

"Thank you so much." Melba flipped through

the book. "These recipes look wonderful. I can't wait to try some of them."

Melba laid the book beside her on the sofa. She then shared with Delta everything about the "Nanette Project."

"If you decide you want to help us, I feel it is only fair to tell you about Eddie and his threats."

When Melba explained about Eddie, Delta laughed and said, "If he pulls that stuff with me, I'm gonna say, 'look here, buster, you go messing with this African-American lady, you better watch out. You ever heard of a discrimination lawsuit? If you mess with me, you're sure gonna hear of one.' That'll stop him. I probably couldn't come up with a legitimate lawsuit, but I'll bet I could scare him into behaving. So don't y'all worry about that part of it. I'll take care of Eddie."

"There's another problem, Delta. We can't persuade Nanette to leave her apartment. Except for picking up her meals in the dining room, the only time she ever gets out of it is when she goes somewhere with her son. We know she won't come over to your apartment and you sure can't drag a piano to hers."

Delta chuckled. "You are cooking up problems where there aren't any. No way I could squeeze my big old piano into this tiny apartment, so I sold the piano and bought myself the fanciest keyboard I could find. I can make that thing sound like a whole orchestra. It's portable, so I can take it to Nanette's apartment. All I need is the sheet music and I'm off and running."

"Nanette has stacks of sheet music, so that's sure no problem. You're an angel, Delta, and I am so grateful you'll be helping us with our project."

The others were waiting at the lunch table when Melba arrived. "Yes, I talked to Delta," she said before she even sat down, "and bless her heart, she is as excited as we are. I got so tickled at her."

Melba told the group what Delta has said about Eddie. "I think she was wishing old Eddie would show up and threaten her. She's really a fine woman and she said she'll keep an eye on Nanette and try to persuade her to join her for lunch in the dining room. Isn't that the greatest?"

CHAPTER Fourteen

Delta was true to her word and was a frequent visitor in Nanette's apartment. Also, Stephanie and Jennifer went by as often as they could to keep encouraging and helping Nanette. They had both been concerned about what would happen to the "Nanette Project" when the time came for Stephanie's departure. They decided that Jennifer would come by once a month to trim Nanette's hair. And Delta eagerly offered to see that Nanette kept herself "spruced up" as she put it.

Stephanie made one last visit to Nanette and explained about her new job and promised to phone often for a chat. Nanette gave her a long hug at the door. "I'll miss you, Sweetie."

Several weeks later, Delta reported that Nanette had promised to join her in the dining room for lunch. "We have room at our table. I have already told the others about the 'Nanette Project' and I think they will be very welcoming to Nanette. Also Nanette and I have another surprise we are working on. I can't tell you about that one yet, but it's a good one!"

*****

"Hey, y'all," Melba announced one morning at breakfast. "I saw Delta downstairs and she told me to tell everybody to watch the bulletin boards for a special announcement. I kept bugging her about it until she handed me a preview copy. What do you think?"

She handed the piece of paper to Bertha. Bertha read aloud: "You are invited to a gala social hour in the Gardendale dining room Wednesday, April 21, at 5:30 p.m. Don't miss it. We will have a special guest entertainer."

Evie gasped. "Oh, my goodness! Do you think it could possibly be Nanette?"

"It's got to be Nanette since Delta is the one preparing the posters. That's next Wednesday, just five days from now. And for some scary reason, that reminds me. Has anybody seen Eddie lately?"

"Delta told me he's been coming on weekends to bring frozen dinners and ice cream treats to his mother and apparently he hasn't suspected anything is going on. You'd think he would be suspicious since she's been looking so much better, but I guess he either doesn't notice or doesn't care. Either way, it's good for us. He must not think the 'meddling old biddies' are messing around with his mother anymore."

By 5:30 on Wednesday afternoon, the dining room was full and everybody had been served punch or a glass of wine along with some light snacks. Just as the residents were wondering who the mystery guest could be, Delta entered through the main door of the dining room and strode purposefully to the center of the room where her keyboard was set up. She picked up the microphone and pushed the "on" button.

"Ladies and gentlemen, as many of you know, I am Delta Alexander and a resident of The Gardendale. It is my great pleasure tonight to introduce to you one of our own talented residents who will sing some of your favorite melodies from your and my youth. Please, let's give a big welcome to the lovely Nanette Wilson."

At that moment Nanette swept through the main door to the applause of the audience. Her red dress, its top glittering with reflections from the chandelier overhead, fell in soft folds over her slim figure, and with her hair and makeup perfect, she seemed to float to the center of the room. With gracious poise, she accepted the microphone from Delta and stood smiling confidently while Delta played the introduction to 'So Glad I Found You.' Nanette began:

So glad I found you,
It's heaven with my arms around you
The years that I searched just for you
Weren't in vain...

Nanette was every inch the pro as she sang the song without missing a note, her voice sultry, her face glowing with happiness.

"Oh, no. Oh, no," Sally whispered to her friends. "Look who just came in the side door looking like a thundercloud. It's Eddie. Oh, please, please, Eddie, don't ruin this for your mother. Pray, girls, like you've never prayed before," and they did, their hearts pounding. "Please, God, don't let him destroy this moment for Nanette."

Eddie stood transfixed staring at his mother and later the friends had a hard time describing what happened next. His whole demeanor changed and his expression softened as he watched her. She still had not caught sight of him.

Eddie waited until she finished the song, then walked over to his mother. He was beside her before she realized he was there. He stepped in front of her and opened his arms and they embraced. Only then did those sitting nearby notice that Eddie had tears in his eyes.

Melba dug a tissue from her pocket and wiped her eyes. "Look around the room, y'all. I'll bet there's not a dry eye in this place."

When Eddie stepped back from his mother, she said into the microphone, "I would like to introduce to you my son Eddie, who has given me a joyful surprise by being here tonight. I would like to dedicate my next song to Eddie. Ready, Delta?"

With that, Delta began the intro to "Memories" and Nanette sang the old favorite with a joy in her voice that was a gift to everybody in the room.

After several more numbers, Nanette and Delta

sat at the table with Eddie to drink some punch and take a break. Eddie excused himself from the table. "I'll be back in a minute, Mom. There's something I have to do."

"Uh, oh," Evie warned. "Here comes Eddie."

Eddie pulled a chair up to the table. "May I sit for just a moment? I know you ladies are behind all that is happening here tonight. I have my spies, too. There is something I need to say to you.

"First of all, I need to ask you if crow will be on the menu anytime soon because if it is I want to come eat with you." The women laughed and their fear disintegrated.

Evie said, "They won't be serving crow, but we would love for you to come have lunch with us anytime."

Eddie continued, "I have done you a disservice and I hope you will forgive me. When I was a child, my mom had to make a choice--stay with the band and travel or stay home with her child. She chose me. I remember when I was just a little boy, my dad took me to hear mom sing in a hotel nightclub. She had on that same red dress and I thought she was the most beautiful and glamorous mother anybody could ever have. And that's how she looked tonight--beautiful and glamorous and happy. I think I overreacted to your ministering to her because I was frightened at seeing her grow old and change and I was afraid that somehow you might hurt her and I needed to protect her. But you have been fairy godmothers to her and I thank you from the bottom of my heart." He rose and headed back to his mother's table as Delta and Nanette prepared to finish the program.

"How's that for an answer to our prayers?" asked Sally. "Who could ask for anything more?"

Melba laughed. "Maybe Nanette will sing that one next!"

CHAPTER Fifteen

Spring had come to The Gardendale and the courtyards were bursting with the pinks of redbuds and azaleas. Great golden arcs of forsythia spilled over onto the walkways. The four friends were sipping lemonade around a wrought iron table in one of the shady garden gazebos.

Anyone walking by and taking a casual look at the group would have seen nothing unusual, just four typical "old ladies" enjoying the warm spring air. Except for their ubiquitous white hair, the four in fact were quite different, even in appearance.

Melba was petite, pretty, and almost doll-like. Her children and grandchildren doted on her and she basked in their loving attention, even encouraging it with an attitude of helplessness. Her friends knew better and were amused by her "little girl" affectations and how adroitly she managed to get her way. A problem with her balance required Melba's use of a walker, but the walker was such a part of her that people hardly noticed it, somewhat like eyeglasses that become a part of one's face.

Bertha, the oldest of the four, looked much younger than her eighty-nine years. She was tall and slender, with a straight-backed posture that attested to her athletic interest and ability, for in fact, she still participated with her bowling league in their weekly competitions. She was an avid baseball fan and even kept up with the statistics of her favorite players.

Sally was the quietest and most introspective of the group. The few freckles sprinkled across her cheeks hinted at the redhead she once was. Her quiet nature belied the image of the fiery temper that was supposed to accompany red hair. She could remember having a temper, but she supposed that as the red hair turned into cool, snowy white, perhaps the temper, too, cooled off.

Evie was "five four and shrinking" as she put it. She was in a constant battle with osteoporosis and currently, with new medications, felt she was winning the battle. Her brown eyes sparkled with humor, but she could also pop with anger when provoked. The others tried to be careful not to cross her and invoke her ire.

"I absolutely love this time of year," Bertha declared, sipping her icy lemonade. "Cool mornings, afternoons warm enough to enjoy the pool, and then cool evenings that are great for walking."

"Yeah," agreed Melba, "it's my favorite time, too."

Evie picked up a paper napkin and wiped at the moisture on her lemonade glass. "By the way, Bertha, speaking of springtime reminds me, you have a birthday coming up in a month. Any special plans?"

"I guess the usual--dinner out with the family. My daughters usually take me to my favorite dress shop and tell me to pick out anything I want and then we have lunch at the tearoom in the Village. That's always fun."

"There's something else you were going to do this birthday since it's the big nine oh, something you've been promising your family for several years now," said Evie.

"I can't imagine what you're talking about," said Bertha, looking genuinely puzzled.

"Bertha, don't you remember? You promised them and us, too, that you would stop driving when you reached the age of 90."

"Oh, that. I've changed that to 95. I've decided that since I am still a good driver and my eyesight is still good and I haven't had any accidents, there's no need to give up driving. Besides, every time I turn on that ignition, I ask God to get me safely to wherever I'm going and He always does."

"Always?" rejoined Evie. "You say 'no accidents,' but what about that horrible accident last fall when your car was totaled?"

"Well, as you recall, that accident was not my fault. That girl in the pickup truck ran the red light and broadsided me. Lordy, I can still hear that awful crunching sound when that truck plowed into me.

She spun my car around and into another car. Other people stopped their cars and came running over to me asking if I wanted them to call an ambulance. Seeing the extent of the damage, they were sure I had to be badly injured."

Sally spoke up, "Your accident was exactly the same as my Jacob's and he was killed. I don't understand how you weren't injured."

"Truthfully, I don't either. Anyway, these people kept asking to call an ambulance for me and they did call the police. But I insisted I was just fine--and I was. I got out of the car and no part of my body hurt, not even a little bit. I called my son on my cell phone and when he got there, he couldn't believe it either. He wanted to at least take me to a doctor."

"Mom," he told me, "there's no way you can be in an accident this bad and not be injured."

"He finally relented and let me have my way, but insisted I would be really sore the next day. Well, I wasn't and I haven't had even a twinge from that accident."

"I still don't see how you can say God got you safely to your destination that day," said Evie, "when your car was completely totaled."

With exasperation in her voice, Bertha answered, "Evie, it has to be a miracle I wasn't hurt. My answer to you is that God got me safely to my destination just as I asked Him to for whatever reason He had. It just never occurred to me to ask Him to get my car there safely, too!"

Evie laughed. "Good point, Bertha. So maybe it's not yet time to give up driving."

"Do you think we're the best friends in this whole place?" Melba suddenly asked.

The others looked puzzled. "What do mean?" asked Bertha. "I don't understand what you are asking."

"Well, there are lots of best friends in this place. But are we the BEST best friends here?"

They were still puzzled, but Evie answered, "Of course we are. How many other friends here have plotted to blow up a leaf blower, for goodness sake? You can't get much more "best friends" than that! Even though our friendships have ups and downs, or maybe I should say 'up the streets' and 'down the streets,' the bond endures. And trust me, Melba, our being friends is one of the things that helps me plod on through the years."

Sally spoke up. "Every time I think about that leaf blower, I feel guilty. Do the rest of you feel that way? You know, we really did do something wrong even if it all turned out all right."

"I'm glad you brought that up," said Melba, "because I, too, have felt bad about trying to blow up that thing. We stole something and we destroyed somebody else's property and anyway you slice it, those are bad things."

"Well, then," said Evie, "why don't we do something about it? I think Mr. Jones knows who did it anyway, but let's all go confess to him and offer to pay for the new blower they had to buy."

"Good idea," agreed Melba. "It would sure make me feel better to get that vandalism off my chest. In fact, let's put this lemonade in my apartment and go right now before we lose our nerve. Let's hope he's in his office."

After Melba took the tray of lemonade into her kitchen, they marched off to the office. Mr. Jones happened to be out in the reception area of the office handing a piece of paper to the secretary. "Hello, ladies. How are you today?"

"We need to speak with you privately," said Evie. "We promise it won't take long."

Mr. Jones ushered them into his private office and closed the door. "Please sit down," he said, motioning to the small loveseat and two chairs in his office. He seated himself behind his desk. "Now, what can I do for you?"

Melba spoke up before anyone else could say anything. "I should be the one to confess because I am the one who made the bomb and ruined the leaf blower and we are the ones who plotted it and we feel guilty and would like to pay for the new leaf blower that you had to buy."

"We were all in on it, not just Melba, so we are all to blame," said Evie. "And the bomb was my idea."

Mr. Jones stared at them. "Bomb? There was a bomb?"

"Well," said Melba, "it was supposed to be a bomb, but it turned out to be a dessert, but it ruined the leaf blower anyway and we would feel much better if you would let us pay for the new one."

Mr. Jones rested his elbows on his desk and tapped his fingers together tent-style. "Well, ladies, I appreciate your coming in to tell me what you did, but the matter is all settled and the leaf blower bought and paid for. But, how about this? I will tell you how much the leaf blower cost us and you can donate that amount to one of the charities that The Gardendale residents support."

"That sounds good," said Sally. "We'll bring the check to you so you can see that we are making the donation. Thank you so much for helping us to ease our consciences. We're not really bad people, you know."

Mr. Jones smiled. "Believe me, I know that. I know about some of your 'projects' here that have brought happiness to people and I am grateful to have you as residents. But you might want to think twice before you decide to set off any more bombs."

"Oh, boy, he's right about that," Evie said as they left the Director's office. "Who would think that four old ladies could get into so much trouble? I say, no more. Let's behave from now on." They strolled along in silence for a few minutes when Bertha exclaimed, "Nah. That's no fun. Let's hunt up another project."

"All right," said Melba enthusiastically and the others agreed. "I hear there have been more thefts lately and I'll bet we can figure out who the culprit is."

CHAPTER Sixteen

Later, in the quiet of her apartment, Sally thought about the thefts. Solving the mystery would engage her mind and divert it from moping around as she had been doing lately.

Sally hadn't told her friends, but to keep her mind busy and try to get it off some concerns she had, she had been attempting to write a book. Many years earlier she had taken a writing course in college and enjoyed it, so she decided writing again might give her something to do to fill some of the empty hours in her life.

She had dug through her desk drawers until she found the small tape recorder she had bought to play music on. It was a cheap thing and the sound was terrible for music, but not too bad for recording someone talking, so she had hung onto it. She put in fresh batteries and was pleased that it would still work. Now she could keep it handy so that when she had an idea for the story, she could dictate into the recorder, then transcribe it later.

Last night she had inadvertently left it on "record" for the entire length of the tape. This morning when she was ready to transcribe what she had dictated the evening before, she couldn't find that part of the tape containing her dictation. She felt sure that somewhere on the tape she would find what she had dictated, but was having no luck rewinding and fast-forwarding trying to find what she needed. Finally she gave up and decided to play the whole tape from the beginning--a whole hour of her life accidentally recorded on tape.

Sally gathered her quilting supplies to continue work on the quilt she was stitching for her granddaughter. She put the little player on the coffee table and pushed the play button. As she listened, pushing the short quilting needle in and out of the soft fabric, she was struck by the sadness of the sounds or rather of the long silences on the tape, broken only by the ticking of the big grandfather clock her husband had built for her, and now and then, her deep sighs as she had worked on the quilt the evening before. Only once was there another sound, the whirring of the blender as she made a fruit smoothie for her supper. Otherwise, nothing but those sighs and the hypnotic, relentlessly rhythmic voice of the clock. I need to get the chimes repaired, she reminded herself. Even the clock is dying.

On and on the tape played, pointing out to Sally

her aloneness in a way she was never before aware of. That silence, punctuated only by her sighs and the slow, quiet tick tick tick of her life moving inexorably toward its end, saddened her to the core of her being. It made her loneliness so real, so penetrating, so there.

No wonder many of the people in this haven for the aged played their televisions from dawn until they went to bed at night. Sally enjoyed her TV only if the programming was particularly heart lightening or interesting, but to have it on all the time would have made her nuts so she settled for the silence.

Sally remembered the time Bertha asked Melba about talking to herself and Melba defended herself vigorously and well. Sally knew she, too, often talked to herself, but she didn't want to admit it. Truth to tell, it did worry her just a bit because she had always heard that people who talked to themselves were crazy. Was she crazy? Was she going crazy? Would her mind disintegrate before her body? Who was she anymore, anyway--this woman whose home used to be full of children banging their way in and out, laughter--lots of laughter--phones and doorbells ringing, a loving husband's voice, "Hi, I'm home," her own voice humming and singing old songs off key. Tears came to her eyes.

I have got to get out of here, she thought, and fast. This could be a whopper of a pity party. Sally put on her walking shoes and sweater and locked the door behind her. Her own cure when reality crashed down on her was to go outside and walk round and round the complex. She had heard someone say that three times around is a mile. Sometimes it took more than that to restore her soul, but it did seem to work. Thank goodness she was able to walk without difficulty when so many of the residents here couldn't. Sally thanked God for this blessing.

As she walked, she began to think about the thefts. It was unnerving and frightening to know that now jewelry, clothing, even small household items were disappearing from the residents' apartments. Maybe Melba was right--solving the crime would give them something to do.

CHAPTER Seventeen

Thursday mornings were French toast time at The Gardendale. Warm maple-flavored syrup made the rounds and Maricela brought a fresh pot of coffee for the table.

"What's the news?" asked Bertha. "I spent yesterday shopping with my daughter and didn't get home until 8:30 last night. This place is totally deserted after dinner in the evening. Talk about rolling up the sidewalks!"

"Then you didn't hear about Leila, did you?" Melba asked as she poured a generous helping of syrup over her toast.

"No. Did something happen to Leila?"

"Yep," answered Melba. "Died playing bingo. Her caregiver rolled Leila's wheelchair to the dining room and parked it at Leila's usual place, then left. Leila was playing three bingo cards and seemed to be enjoying herself when all of a sudden she put her head down on the table like she was sleepy or something. Never made a sound, just as quiet as a mouse. Turned out she died right then and there."

"Wow!" said Bertha. "I guess if we could all choose a way to go, that would be it."

"Yeah, I think we all agree that's a pretty good way to go," said Evie. Sally nodded, but remained quiet.

"Uh, oh, excuse me," Bertha said, jumping up from her chair and hurrying to a nearby table. They watched as she bent down and reached for something under the table where Mindy, the lone occupant of the table, was sitting.

"What was that about?" Evie asked when Bertha returned to her seat.

"Oh, Lordy, it seems like everybody in this place is going downhill fast. I saw Mindy getting really agitated about something so I figured I had better get over there to see if I could help before she went into panic mode. Well, when I got there and asked what was the matter, she said she couldn't find her foot, that it was missing."

"Her *foot* was missing?" Evie asked incredulously.

"That's what she said. I decided she thought it was missing because she couldn't see it. It was behind that fat table leg. So I reached down and pulled her foot out from behind the leg of the table and said, 'See, Mindy, here is your foot, right at the end of your leg where it's supposed to be.' That seemed to calm her down."

"Her foot was missing," mused Evie. "Poor old thing. How old is Mindy, anyway? Do any of you know?"

"I heard she's ninety-four," said Bertha. "She's a little addled, but she gets around well--doesn't even use a cane or walker."

"Diapers, diapers, diapers! I'm sick of hearing about diapers," Melba exploded. "Just sick and tired of it."

Evie sighed. "Melba, what are you talking about? Diapers?"

"Yes, I think everybody in the news media hates old people. We are being discriminated against."

"How's that?" asked Bertha.

"You know all that stuff in the news about that movie actress who wore adult disposable underwear so she wouldn't have to stop at a restroom when she was traveling? She was chasing her boyfriend who had run off with another woman. Well, nobody would even have known about the so-called diapers if she hadn't been in an accident. Those sneering media people and the comedians on TV, too, seem to delight in talking only about the 'diapers' she wore." Melba's eyes snapped with anger.

"If they absolutely must mention them it would be kinder to all the elderly people who have to wear them to call them adult disposable underwear or protective underwear or whatever they're called on the package they come in. I hope every single one of those insensitive media people ends up wearing 'diapers' when they get old."

"I agree," said Bertha. "It would serve them right."

"Hmm," said Sally. "All this talk about underwear reminds me of what my cousin told me one time. Right after he finished college he got a job teaching Junior High math way back in the hills and "hollers" of the Appalachian Mountains. He told me this as the actual truth. Some of those mamas would sew their kids into their winter underwear and not un-sew it until spring. Of course, those union suits had flaps they could open for personal needs."

"You can't be serious!" Evie said. "They would stay in those things all winter? He must have been pulling your leg."

"No, it was the truth. You have to remember this was a long time ago. I'm sure that's not still the case. It's just that they were so isolated with no running water or electricity that they just lived more primitively.

"I may have told you that my sister was a public health nurse in that same area. One day she was in a woman's house to see a sick child and the woman ran outside when a plane flew over. When she came back in the house she said to my sister, 'I hope someday I get to see one of them critters on the ground.'"

"Don't you think having electricity and especially television will have changed the way they live and think?" asked Evie.

"Probably. I only hope it hasn't corrupted them. They were good people with tightly-knit families who really cared about each other. I would hate to think that has changed."

"Dadgum," said Bertha, "there it goes again right in the middle of breakfast, somebody's cell phone ringing with that obnoxious music, but I never see anybody answer it."

"It's Nellie's," said Evie. "She has more friends than a dog has fleas and they seem to call her whenever the mood hits them even in the middle of meals."

"But it couldn't be Nellie with the cell phone. She walks in here empty handed every day and her pockets don't bulge, so where's her cell phone?"

Melba's face lighted up. "So that's why Nellie's chest plays music all the time and she leaves the dining room."

"Yeah," laughed Evie. "She keeps her cell phone tucked into her bra. You would never know it's there except for the ringing. And she can't very well go digging around for it in here, so she goes out into the hall to answer her phone."

"Well, that's one mystery solved," Bertha said, as she poured herself some fresh coffee.

"This place gets kookier all the time," muttered Sally. "What next?"

"I wonder if I have already lived the worst day of my life," said Melba as she poured creamer into her coffee. "Do you ever wonder that?"

"I guess that's 'what's next,' Sally," Evie whispered.

"My gosh, Melba, how do you come up with these things?" asked Bertha. "To answer your question, I sure know what the worst day of my life was and I hope and pray that I never have another day anything like that one."

"It was the day Mattie died, wasn't it?" asked Evie. "That's my worst day, too, the day Allan died of pneumonia. It all happened so fast. He was only seven years old and was fine and happy and healthy, and then, suddenly he was so sick he died. As hard as it was to lose my husband, losing my child was the most horrible thing ever."

Everyone was quiet, each thinking about her own worst time.

CHAPTER Eighteen

Strolling back to her apartment in the spring sunshine, Sally thought back to her "worst time." The memory would never leave her; she believed if she could lose that memory she would count it a blessing. She tried to keep thoughts of that horrendous day suppressed She wanted more than anything to keep the good memories of her son fresh, to remember how excited he was about the family's plans to get together in a few days to celebrate his thirtieth birthday, but now and then something would trigger the memory of that awful day. Sally entered her apartment, sat down before her computer and opened the file labeled "My Journal." She had begun keeping the journal shortly after Jacob died because the counselor in her grief group said that journaling could help.

She looked at the date of the first entry, twelve

years ago, twelve whole years since that worst of days. She read what she had written a few weeks after Jacob died.

> I don't think I will ever "get over it." I know I won't. If the memories of that blackest of all days will just recede some and fade some, it will help. That day..........
>
> From somewhere down in the very depths of my soul, from the deepest, darkest, most frightening part I had never known was there, came a voice crying out to God, "No, no, no," over and over and over again. Even as I knew it was true, it couldn't be true. Our wonderful, full-of-joy-and-humor son COULD NOT POSSIBLY BE DEAD. "No, no, NO." I heard the voice twisting up and out of me and filling the room as I sank to the stairs holding the railing as though it were a life preserver that would save me from the boulder that was my heart and that was drowning me in such pain.
>
> Mark was so pale. He had spent the last hour since we were told of the accident trying to get details, trying to get someone somewhere to tell us something. We couldn't even find out where our son had been taken. "No, sir. I am sorry. We have no information in our computer. Are you sure he was being brought to University Hospital?"
>
> "Please connect me with the emergency

room." Same answer. "Please let me speak to the doctor in charge of the emergency room."

And when he was finally connected to the ER physician, Mark insisted that we be told if our son was alive. "We are 90 miles away. We need to know now if Jacob is alive or not."

"I am sorry to give you bad news on the telephone, sir, but he died at the scene."

As I write this, some seven weeks later, tears pour down my cheeks and sobs still shake my body. And I still cannot fully accept the fact that Jacob is gone, that our son is DEAD, (what a final, bitter word, a word so acrid for one who believes in an after-life of sweet joy.) I cannot accept the fact that Jenny is without her husband who adored her so deeply and who gave her credit for so much of the joy in his life. I cannot accept the fact that little Jacob will never know his dad, the dad who was so extremely proud of his son, only five months old when his daddy was killed. There it is again, KILLED, in one of those horrible, twisted-metal collisions that you read about or see on TV but which surely will never happen to someone you love.

Sally stared at the screen. What she had written would probably sound maudlin and overdramatic to anyone reading it. In her younger years a professor had written at the top of one of her papers, "You have a tendency to gush." Is this what he meant? At the time of his comment she had been stung and wanted to answer the professor, "Well, of course, you jerk. I'm Southern so what do you expect?" But wisely she had kept quiet.

The outpouring in her journal had come straight from her heart at the time she wrote it, the time when the pain was still a physical ache in her chest. And if she were writing it now for the first time, the words would not change. Besides, this was written for her eyes and for her heart only.

Sally closed the file. She sat in front of the computer screen, still and quiet. If anyone had asked her what she was doing, she would have answered simply, "sorrowing."

The pain never really leaves. It just hides under the daily activities and living of life. The sorrow is always there, waiting to pounce on you and envelop you in darkness.

The computer screen saver came to life and the banner on its continuous journey across the screen read "Count Your Blessings." How can there be any blessing in such a horrendous event? When the accident happened, Sally searched for a blessing and all she could find was that Jacob died instantly without suffering and that up until that moment he had lived a joyous life. I believe with all my heart that his spirit is in a better place, she told herself once more. Yes, those were blessings and she thanked God for them.

When Jacob died, Sally wanted to die, too, but gradually the healing began and now she tried to live her life to the fullest. Round and round we go, she said to herself. She once more thought about the possibility of her own death and the prospect of joining her husband and child and other loved ones. Now that possibility was closer and she was wondering if and how much she should tell her friends.

CHAPTER Nineteen

"Where is Evie?" asked Bertha. "She knows we were going to meet today and I'm sure she knows we are supposed to get together here in my apartment. Wonder if I should call her. Evie's never late."

The Bomb Squad was meeting once more, this time in Bertha's apartment. "I hate to start without Evie and besides, her being late worries me because she is always so prompt and now she is ten minutes late."

At that moment, the doorknocker sounded. "Come on in," Bertha called. "The door's unlocked." The apartment door opened and Evie limped into the room, obviously in pain.

Bertha eased out of her chair and went to Evie. "Oh, my gosh. What's the matter?"

Evie winced as she took a step. "I got run over."
"Run over? You're kidding! When? Where?"

"Just now, right outside the elevator. It was Margaret and her blasted scooter. You know how she drives straight into the elevator and then when she gets off, she backs straight out, never checking to see if anybody is behind her. We all know to get out of her way. But this time, I was talking to somebody and my back was turned to the elevator. I heard the doors open, but the scooter is so quiet, I didn't hear it and she banged right into my leg. It hurts like the devil, but I guess it will be all right. I'll probably just have a big bruise for a while. Durn reckless driver," she muttered as she limped to a chair and sat herself down.

Her friends all agreed they would be more watchful of Margaret on her scooter. "We are glad you're at least able to walk, Evie," Sally said, sympathy in her voice. "It's a good thing she didn't knock you down. You could have broken some bones."

"Are you sure that chair is comfortable for you, Evie? I can get you a little footstool if that would help."

"No, I'm fine and ready to find out what we are going to do."

"My thinking is that we need to make a plan," Bertha said, "if we are going to try to solve the thefts. First of all we have to find out if there is a pattern in these thefts. I've made a list of the people I know of who have had things stolen. You add anybody you know of and then we'll interview them. What do you think we should ask them?"

"I think we should try to find out when the residents were gone, when they missed the stolen objects, and also what the stolen items were," said Evie. "There could be a pattern in there somewhere. Maybe the thief only steals things that can be fenced by a jeweler or maybe he only steals stuff that can be sold at a flea market."

"Good thinking, Evie," said Bertha. "Everybody, when you do your interviews be sure to take notes, especially about times and dates. I'll get copies of the activity calendars for the past several months and we can check the theft dates against those."

Melba spoke up. "We need to keep in mind that the thefts wouldn't necessarily be discovered right away and that could throw us off."

"True," agreed Bertha, "but we have to start somewhere and I guess this is as good a place as any. Let's start by all of us making lists of everybody we can think of who has had things go missing in the last few months. We'll meet here again in a couple of days and see what we have come up with."

*****

"I wonder what Sally's up to." Evie sprinkled generous amounts of salt and pepper on her scrambled eggs. "She missed lunch yesterday and she told me she wouldn't be here today either. There's something Sally's not telling us and it worries me. I wasn't going to say anything, but yesterday after breakfast I saw her waiting out front where they pick up residents for the medical run. I didn't actually see her get on the bus, but it sure looked like that was where she was headed."

"Do you think you should tell her you saw her and ask her what's going on?" asked Melba.

"No, let's just leave it alone for now. Sally's very private about things like that and she'll probably tell us in her own good time."

"Well," said Melba defiantly, "I'm going to ask her anyway, no matter what you say. She needs to know we care about her. And if it upsets her I'm sorry."

The next morning Melba did indeed ask Sally as soon as they were served their breakfasts and were beginning to eat. "Sally, are you okay? We've been worried about you."

"I'm fine," Sally answered quietly. Then visibly upset, she abruptly rose from the table and picked up her door keys. "I'm sorry, but please excuse me," and she hastily left the dining room.

"Oh, my gosh, I really messed up that time."

"Don't worry about it, Melba. I have a feeling Sally is going to confide in us soon. You can only keep such strong concerns and feelings bottled up for so long, then it usually spills out. We'll all be here for her when it does. Meanwhile, let's just try to keep our conversations upbeat."

Sally rejoined the group for breakfast the next day. As soon as they were all there and settled into their seats, Sally said, "I need to tell you something." She paused to be sure they were all listening and she could speak softly. "I know you wonder where I've been lately. Well, I have had several medical appointments. You see, I have breast cancer. Before you say anything, the doctor thinks they have caught it quite early, but I'll have surgery in ten days and then we'll know more, like whether they will have to remove the breast. All they have done so far is biopsy a lump which proved to be malignant."

The group was silent, stunned at Sally's announcement. Finally Bertha spoke.

"Sally, if it will make you feel any better, I've been there, done that, double mastectomy. Bet you thought these bodacious ta-tas, as my daughter calls them, were home-grown but they're store-bought."

Her three friends gaped at Bertha.

"You're kidding," said Sally. "You've had breast cancer and you never told us?"

"Well, it was so long ago that I don't really think about it much anymore. It was so far back that implants weren't that common so I just buy my prostheses at a shop. I've been waiting for years for somebody to say, 'Oh, stuff it, Bertha,' so I can answer, 'I do--every day.'"

Bertha's friends laughed.

"There's been no recurrence of the cancer, so I stopped worrying about it a long time back. And it's not the kind of thing where you say, please pass the salt, guess what, I had breast cancer. I dare say if you questioned all the women in this room right now, you'd find that I'm far from being the only one who has had breast cancer."

"Also, Sally," added Evie, "the options and treatments are so much better now than they used to be. And never forget, we are all here for you all the time, whenever you need us."

"I am so glad I told you. Just sharing it with you makes me feel better and you in turn have given me a good dose of optimism. I promise I will keep you posted on everything."

On Monday, two days before Sally's surgery, the Bomb Squad again met at Bertha's. They sat at Bertha's dining table armed with recent activity calendars and copies of the data on the thefts.

"Okay, everybody look for some kind of pattern," Bertha urged. "I just know it's here."

They studied the information for a few minutes until Evie looked at her watch and said, "I've got to go. There's a food committee meeting in ten minutes and I'm chairman so I have to be there. Why don't we take all this home with us and think about it?"

*****

"Sally's surgery is this morning at nine," Bertha told the others at breakfast on Wednesday. "She stayed at her daughter Susie's most of yesterday and then checked into the hospital yesterday afternoon. I asked Susie if she would like for any of us to come sit with her during the surgery, but she said she had other family who would wait with her. She'll call me as soon as they know anything and I'll call you when I get some news. Sure hope it all goes okay."

"I think I feel more nervous and apprehensive

about her surgery than Sally does," said Melba.

"Don't let that cool and calm act fool you. Sally is scared and nervous, too, but anxious to have the whole thing over with, whatever the result."

Later that morning Bertha received the phone call she had been waiting for. It was Susie. "Mom came through just fine," she reported, "and we are so relieved. They didn't have to remove her breast, just did a lumpectomy. Everything looks good; the area around the lump is clean and there is no involvement in the lymph nodes. Mom has several options for her post-surgical treatment so she is going to look at the options and probably make a decision in a week or so."

"What are the options?" asked Bertha.

"Well, first of all, they think she can get by without chemotherapy so that leaves four: the first is to do nothing. With that one they predict the cancer could return within ten years and if it does, they will treat it then. The second option is a short concentrated course of radiation. Third is a longer, less concentrated course of radiation, and the fourth option is to take one of the new cancer drugs for five years. I think Mom will be scared of that one since it depletes the bones and she already has a problem with that.

"Mom is still groggy, but when she is more alert, she will be so happy, especially when she learns she didn't have to have a mastectomy and that she won't have to have a long siege of chemotherapy. I think the prospect of chemo bothered her more than anything."

"Susie, thank you so much for calling. Give Sally our love and I'll call the others and tell them the good news the minute I hang up."

CHAPTER Twenty

The news about Sally spread rapidly and her friends rejoiced that the cancer had not spread and that the treatment options seemed to be fairly benign ones. They arranged among themselves to pick up her meals for her and take them to her apartment while she recuperated. Also they were eager to run errands or do whatever else was needed.

As soon as Sally felt up to it, they gathered again to discuss the mystery, this time in Sally's apartment.

When they were seated, Sally announced, "I think I have the answer to how the thief knows when the occupant will be out of the apartment. With all this waiting around I have had to do, I've had time to think about it. Do you remember Edgar Allan Poe's short story 'The Purloined Letter?'"

"I remember vaguely," said Evie, "something

about the letter being in plain sight all the time."

"That's right. In the story, one of the queen's ministers has stolen a letter from her which could be damaging to her so he is blackmailing her with it. The police need to find the letter so they search the minister's hotel suite. They search everywhere and even rip off the wallpaper to see if the letter is hidden underneath. They go so far as to examine the furniture for hollow legs where a letter could be rolled up and hidden inside. When they can't find the letter, they call the famed amateur detective Auguste Dupin. Monsieur Dupin finds the letter and guess where?"

"Oh, it's frustrating," said Evie. "I can't remember. Where does he find it?"

Sally answered, "All the time it has been in plain sight of everybody, which Monsieur Dupin figures out. On the wall is a cheap letter rack hanging from a soiled ribbon. Several letters are in the rack and there among them is the incriminating letter. The minister has attempted to disguise the letter, but Dupin sees through his efforts. So, the solution of how our thief knows which apartment to go to is the same thing."

Nobody spoke until Melba asked, "How? We don't have a letter rack. I just don't get it."

"Ah, but we do have a place right in front of our noses where anybody can find out who isn't home. What do we do before every Gardendale-sponsored trip?"

"The sign-up sheets! Of course!" Evie said.

"How could we not have thought of that? Every time anybody goes anywhere on one of the Gardendale buses, they sign up in the activity room where anybody and everybody can see that they will be gone."

"Right. So the thief can just pick his time. Remember how we found that most of the thefts occurred when the residents were out for the evening. You may remember the old saying from Euripides, 'The day is for honest men, the night for thieves.'"

"Sure enough, our thief wants the cover of darkness, so he checks the calendar for an evening activity like dinner or even better a concert or play that will take a resident away for a whole evening, then he checks on the sign-up sheet for that activity and he knows exactly who will not be here. We even make it more convenient for him by writing our apartment number right beside our name!"

"So how do we catch him?" Bertha wondered aloud.

"I have thought about that, too. See what you think of this plan. We will need some help from the staff, especially the Activities Director. We need to persuade Kim to make up a phony evening trip. We could have only a few people sign up for it so that we would have fewer apartments to watch. The residents in those apartments will actually go downstairs and get on the bus and be driven away. Then we can have residents who are neighbors keep a watch on those apartments and notify security the minute they see anything or anyone suspicious. I know there's only a slim chance we will catch the thief, but I can't come up with a better way."

"It might work," said Evie, "but why does the trip need to be phony? We don't want to make it too easy for him to figure out it's all a setup."

"You're right. So let's make it a real outing. No harm in that. We just need to be sure to limit the number who can go so that we don't have too many apartments to watch."

"Kim can help us figure that out, I'm sure. Maybe she could have only five or six tickets to a concert or something. She's a sharp cookie. If she goes along with our plan, she'll make it all sound very legitimate."

*****

The next day Kim told Sally that she had wangled six tickets to a musical program at the university the next week and that she knew of several people who she thought would like to go. Should she announce it at lunch and let the tickets go to the first six people to sign up? This was agreed upon and the first step toward the trap was set.

Sally informed the Bomb Squad of the plan. To their delight, all six tickets were claimed before the day was out. Bertha and Evie went to the Activity Room to check the sign-out sheet and see who had signed up and would be away that evening. They decided it would be only fair for those six people to know what was going on and to understand that someone would be assigned to watch their apartment that evening.

Bertha jotted down three of the names and Evie took the other three. They returned to their apartments and made the calls. The residents involved were excited to be a part of the hoped-for capture of the thief even though they would be in the theater when it happened.

The next step was to line up people who could watch the empty apartments. The Bomb Squad itself split into pairs and each pair selected an apartment to surveil. All that remained was to find eight more people, so that each of the other four apartments could be watched by two people. Finding these additional people was easier than they had expected and by the end of yet another day, everything was set to go.

Kim would have the bus out front at seven-thirty and the group would be gone by seven-forty-five. The lookouts would be in place by eight even though it would not be truly dark for another thirty minutes or so.

The ladies had confided in Mr. Jones and he not only approved of the plan, he made arrangements for an extra security guard to be on the property in case one was needed. The four friends really appreciated this. The criminal could be armed and dangerous and they surely did not want anybody to get hurt.

Ruby, one of their exercise companions, lived in the apartment Bertha and Evie were going to use and was happy to have the company they provided while the two friends did their watching.

Evie tapped the handle of the door knocker against its brass plate. "It's us, Ruby," she called out as the door opened a crack. "We're here for spy duty."

"Come on in," Ruby welcomed them excitedly. "I've been looking forward to this. I hope we're the ones who catch this burglar. Wouldn't that be something? I've moved some chairs close to the front window so you can easily see straight across the courtyard to the apartment you're going to watch."

"This is perfect, Ruby," Bertha said as she lowered herself into one of the chairs. "We have a great view from here. Thank you so much for letting us use your apartment."

"Are you kidding? This place can be pretty boring sometimes, so I am glad to be in on this. But I have a question. How will you know if anybody suspicious is spotted somewhere else on the property?"

"That's one of the first things we made sure of," answered Evie. "We don't want to miss out on all the action. Of course, each of the watchers has agreed not to set foot outside until it is all over. So this could be a long and very quiet evening. But if anything does happen, the security people have promised to telephone us right away and keep us informed. So, not to worry, we'll know what's going on."

The ladies chatted and caught up on Gardendale news as the darkness deepened. Bertha and Evie watched together sitting side by side, with Ruby's apartment darkened so that they would not be noticed by anyone outside. Fortunately, even though it was dark, they could easily see the outside doorways because each apartment doorway was well lighted for the safety and convenience of the residents.

After a bit, they took turns watching to keep the job from being so tedious. But all was quiet and nothing was happening. Bertha yawned and realized she was becoming quite sleepy when the house phone rang.

"This is it, this is it," Ruby said excitedly and jumped for the phone. She grabbed it from its hook and handed it to Bertha.

"Hello, this is Bertha. Really? No kidding? You don't mean it! And he actually had the necklace in his hand? Wow! Okay, thank you so much for letting us know."

"It worked," exulted Bertha. "It actually worked. Alton and Jane are the ones who called security and told them a man was entering the apartment they were watching. Security called the police and the two security guards went up to the apartment and waited outside. The police arrived in nothing flat and they waited until the man hastened out of the apartment. That way they caught the thief with the goods. His pockets were full of all the jewelry he could stuff in them plus a necklace he was holding in his hand."

"Wow! I can't believe it. Who was it? Was it anybody we know?" Evie was firing questions at Bertha.

"Yeah, it was, sort of. Do you remember the lazy maintenance man who hid the leaf blower we stole? Remember, he stuck it behind the pool house so he wouldn't have to put it away while he ate lunch. His name is Clyde. Apparently, he's our thief! They'll tell us more tomorrow.

"Ruby, thanks for letting us borrow your apartment. We did enjoy visiting with you so it was an evening well spent. We'll let you get to bed now. See you tomorrow!"

A called meeting of the residents was quickly scheduled for later the next morning. Everybody was chattering about the events of the night before and all were eager to hear more details.

By the time the meeting began, there was standing room only. Mr. Jones called the meeting to order and the chatter finally died down.

"As I am sure all of you have heard by now, the person who has been breaking into the apartments here has been apprehended. You have probably also heard that the man responsible for the thefts is Clyde, the newest person on the maintenance staff. I will tell you that he has been on probation in his job here at the Gardendale because of his irresponsible handling of his duties, but we had no idea of the extent of his misdeeds.

"Of course, he had a master key which made it quite easy for him to slip into any apartment without being suspected even if he were seen. When his workday was over at 5:30 p.m., he would leave the premises as did the rest of the maintenance staff. Then he would return under cover of darkness.

"He has confessed to all the thefts and we are

very fortunate that he still has most of what he stole and it will eventually be returned to its owners. Seems he is not a seasoned criminal and didn't know how to find a fence for the stolen goods!

"Before we end this meeting, I want to offer my thanks and the thanks of every resident here to the four ladies who solved the mystery and came up with a plan to catch the thief. Would Sally, Bertha, Evie, and Melba please stand up? Let's give them a really big round of applause and I hope that you will individually thank them for helping us out of a most unhappy situation."

*****

Sally, Bertha, Evie, and Melba sat together that evening at the wine and cheese party The Gardendale had each month to honor new residents. Melba held up her glass: "To the best best friends in the world." The others echoed her: "To the best best friends in the world," and they touched their glasses.

Epilogue

Clyde was convicted of burglary and is serving a five-year sentence in the state penitentiary. After the trial, his wife, Bonnie Lou, stated to a reporter: "It serves the bum right. All those burglaries and he never even gave me so much as a bracelet."

Melba signed up to teach English to Spanish-speaking immigrants at a nearby church. Since she often forgets which days she is to teach, the church sends a van to pick her up and her friends make sure she is ready to go each Tuesday and Thursday at 9 a.m.

The Admiral and Lucy Belle are living happily ever after with only a few minor explosions of temper on Lucy Belle's part. The Admiral bought her a big box of Nerf balls to throw at him when her anger gets the best of her. There have been no more fires in their apartment.

Sally's cancer tests continue to be negative and

she is encouraged about the future. She is a faithful volunteer at the local cancer center where she won an award as "Volunteer of the Year."

Evie had successful cataract surgery and can now see all the way across the dining room. She is "going out with" a gentleman who moved into the facility after a long career as a sports equipment salesman. "He's a sweetheart," she says, "but I am getting a little sick of hearing about skis and bats and balls and the best way to prevent your running shoes from being smelly."

Bertha was elected president of the Gardendale Resident Association and stays busy "trying to straighten the place out." She is accused of being bossy and dictatorial, but she says that doesn't bother her one whit. If somebody doesn't like the way she runs things, then, by golly, let them be president!

Nanette and Delta are fast friends and every few months they entertain residents with a concert. Eddie has become a favorite "adopted son" of the residents.

*****

DELTA'S SIX-WEEKS MUFFINS
1 (15oz) box fruit & fiber or other cereal
1 cup melted shortening
4 cups sugar
4 eggs, beaten
1 quart buttermilk
5 cups flour

5 teaspoons baking soda
3 teaspoons salt

In large bowl mix bran, sugar, flour, soda, and salt. Add beaten eggs, shortening, and buttermilk. Mix well. Store in covered container in refrigerator for up to six weeks. Preheat oven to 400 degrees. Fill greased muffin tins 1/2 to 2/3 full. Bake 15 to 20 minutes until muffins break open on top or are lightly browned.

ALSO BY MARCIA BENNETT

BOOKS FOR THE CHILDREN IN YOUR LIFE

MYSTERY AT JACOB'S WELL
Four students are plunged into a mystery as they prepare a science report on caves. An underwater cave deep in an eerie well, a mysterious carved stone, frightening cries, and other strange events envelop the students as they seek to unravel the mystery.

MYSTERY AT SADDLECREEK
Trouble is brewing at Saddlecreek, normally a quiet subdivision of Wimberley in the Texas Hill Country. Who is causing all the vandalism, fire and worry? Four young sleuths undertake a careful, methodical investigation. This time, some of them are suspects.

THE BACKPACK CAT
Because his mother has deserted the family, Daniel is being sent across the country to visit a grandmother he doesn't even know. Bring adventure into your life at any time during the year with Daniel, Gram, and Gram's ugly cat, Feogato.

SOMEBODY LEFT THE DOOR OPEN
A book of wild and wacky poems for children. Meet a cast of whimsical characters in this rhythmic romp through childhood with Peculiar Julia, Savannah Banana, Digital Danny, and Timothy Tumble.

Learn more at:
www.outskirtspress.com/marciabennett

Printed in the United States
109234LV00001B/82-129/P